BY JANET EVANOVICH

The Stephanie Plum novels

One For The Money	Lean Mean Thirteen
Two For The Dough	Fearless Fourteen
Three To Get Deadly	Finger Lickin' Fifteen
Four To Score	Sizzling Sixteen
High Five	Smokin' Seventeen
Hot Six	Explosive Eighteen
Seven Up	Notorious Nineteen
Hard Eight	Takedown Twenty
To The Nines	Top Secret Twenty-One
Ten Big Ones	Tricky Twenty-Two
Eleven On Top	Turbo Twenty-Three
Twelve Sharp	Hardcore Twenty-Four

The Knight and Moon novels

Curious Minds (with Phoef Sutton)

Dangerous Minds

The Fox and O'Hare novels

with Lee Goldberg

The Heist

The Chase

The Job

The Scam

The Pursuit

The Diesel and Tucker series

Wicked Appetite	Wicked Business

Wicked Charms (with Phoef Sutton)

The Between the Numbers Novels

Visions Of Sugar Plums	Plum Lucky
Plum Lovin'	Plum Spooky

And writing with Charlotte Hughes

Full House	Full Speed
Full Tilt	Full Blast

HARDCORE
24

JANET

EVANOVICH

HARDCORE
24

REVIEW

First published in the United States of America in 2017 by
G.P. Putnam's Sons
An imprint of Penguin Random House LLC

First published in Great Britain in 2017 by
HEADLINE REVIEW
An imprint of HEADLINE PUBLISHING GROUP

1

Cataloguing in Publication Data is available from the British Library

ISBN 978 1 4722 4590 8 (Hardback)
ISBN 978 1 4722 4591 5 (Trade Paperback)

Offset in 12.75/18.35 pt Minion Pro by Jouve (UK), Milton Keynes

Printed and bound in Great Britain by Clays Ltd, St Ives plc

Headline's policy is to use papers that are natural, renewable and recyclable
products and made from wood grown in well-managed forests and other
controlled sources. The logging and manufacturing processes are expected
to conform to the environmental regulations of the country of origin.

HEADLINE PUBLISHING GROUP
An Hachette UK Company
Carmelite House
50 Victoria Embankment
London EC4Y 0DZ

www.headline.co.uk
www.hachette.co.uk

HARDCORE
24

ONE

SIMON DIGGERY AND Ethel, his pet boa constrictor, were about fifty feet from Simon's rust bucket double-wide. Ethel looked comfy draped over a branch halfway up the tree. Simon looked like death warmed over. He was scrunched into a crook a couple feet below Ethel. He was barefoot, wearing striped pajamas, and his gray hair was even more of a mess than usual.

My name is Stephanie Plum. I work as a bond enforcement officer in Trenton, New Jersey, and Simon was in violation of his bond.

Simon is a professional grave robber. When he gets caught robbing a grave, my cousin Vinnie is his bail bondsman of choice. Vinnie posts a cash bond guaranteeing the court that if Simon is released he will return when scheduled. If Simon doesn't show up on time, I'm sent out to fetch him.

I was presently standing a respectable distance from the tree, looking up at Simon, keeping a watch on Ethel. I was with my sidekick, Lula.

If Lula was a pastry she'd be a big chocolate cupcake with a lot of frosting. I'd be more of a croissant with a ponytail. I have curly shoulder-length brown hair, blue eyes, and some people think I look like Julia Roberts on her day off.

"Simon," Lula yelled. "What the heck are you and Ethel doing in the tree?"

"I been up here since last night," Simon said. "I'm afraid to come down on account of the zombies."

"You gotta stop drinking that homemade grain liquor," Lula said.

"I wasn't drinking," Simon said. "I was working my trade at that cemetery on Morley Street last night, and I accidentally dug into a zombie portal."

"Say what?" Lula said. "I never heard of no zombie portal."

"It's not widely publicized that they exist. Mostly people in my profession know about it. It's an occupational hazard. I only dug into a portal once before, and I was able to beat the zombies back with my shovel, but this time was a whole other deal. There was too many of them, so I ran for my truck and took off. Only thing is they tracked me down. They got a real good sense of smell. They're like raggedy bloodhounds. They come at me when I was sleeping. They wanted my brain. That's what they kept saying. *Brains, brains, brains.* I'd be a goner if it wasn't for Ethel. She don't like getting woke up, and I guess zombies don't like snakes. Anyways, I was able to get away, and Ethel and me climbed this tree."

"Because zombies can't climb trees?" I asked Simon.

2

"You got it," Simon said. "Zombies only walk straight ahead. They can't back up neither."

"You were supposed to be in court first thing this morning," I told him.

"Well, excuse me," Simon said, "but I had bigger problems. Suppose I was able to get to court, and the zombies followed me there, and they ate all the people's brains who were in the court?"

"This is Trenton," Lula said. "You might not notice."

I cut my eyes to Lula. "There are *no zombies*."

"How can you be sure?" Lula said.

I blew out a sigh and looked back at Simon. "Here's the deal. You come down, and we'll protect you from the zombies."

"You gotta either chop off their head or shoot them in the brain," Simon said. "That's the only way."

"I got a gun," Lula said, shoving her hand into her oversized imitation Jimmy Choo bag. "It's in here somewhere."

"What about Ethel?" Simon said. "If I stay in jail awhile until the zombies forget about me, who's gonna take care of Ethel?"

"You'll have to make arrangements," I said.

"I don't got no one," Simon said. "My cousin Snacker is in West Virginia, and my neighbors would chop her up and fry her in bacon fat. You gotta promise to take care of Ethel."

"No way," I said.

"Me neither," Lula said.

"She's no bother," Simon said. "You just gotta feed her once a week. Just come in and leave her a groundhog or something."

"They don't usually sell groundhog in the supermarket," Lula said.

"I get them from the side of the road," Simon said. "Ethel don't care if they're swelled up or anything. She likes fried chicken too. And she wouldn't stick her nose up at a pizza. And if worse comes to worse I keep a bag of rats in the freezer."

"You got electric?" Lula asked.

"'Course I got electric," Simon said. "This here's a civilized neighborhood."

"How are you going to get Ethel out of the tree?"

"I got some hot dogs," Simon said. "I'll leave a trail of hot dogs that goes straight to the kitchen. And then once she's inside we'll lock the door."

Ten minutes later Simon had the hot dogs all laid out.

"She don't look interested," Lula said, staring up at Ethel.

"It could take a while," Simon said. "She don't move so fast. I guess we could just leave the door open for her."

"You could get robbed if you do that," Lula said.

"I got a fifty-pound snake for a pet," Simon said. "Nobody comes near here excepting the zombies."

I cuffed Simon, promised him I'd look in on Ethel, loaded him into my SUV, and drove him to the police station. I handed him over to the cop in charge, and Simon explained that should a zombie show up, the cop needed to shoot the zombie in the brain. The cop assured Simon it was a done deal.

• • •

It was almost four o'clock when Lula and I got back to Simon's double-wide. The snake wasn't in the tree, and the hot dogs were all gone.

"I'll stand here and keep watch that no one steals your car while you check up on Ethel," Lula said.

"No one's going to steal my car out here," I said. "And I'll take the key."

"Okay then, how about I'm not going anywhere near that snake pit. It got snakes living under it, and it got a giant snake living *in* it. And I don't like snakes. Plus I'm wearing my favorite Via Spigas, and Simon don't keep his walkway up to Via Spiga level."

Lula is a couple inches shorter than me and has about twice as much flesh. Much of the flesh is boob. This week her hair was straightened to the texture of boar bristle, was colored a metallic royal blue, and had been pulled up into a ponytail that stuck out of the top of her head. Between the hair and the heels, she was about seven feet tall. She was wearing a shiny silver tank top with a matching cardigan sweater and a short black skirt. The skirt barely covered her hoo-ha and was stretched out to maximum capacity over her ass. Her spike-heeled Via Spigas matched her hair.

I was in my usual work uniform of running shoes, jeans, sweatshirt, and a fitted V-neck T-shirt. I had a canvas messenger bag slung over my shoulder, and I was wearing La Perla lace bikini panties under my jeans. Not an entirely glamorous outfit, but I was pretty much ready for any emergency.

I carefully approached the double-wide, keeping watch for yard snakes.

"At least you don't have to worry about rats," Lula said. "Nothing a snake likes better than a nice fat rat."

I crept up the makeshift stairs to Simon's door, and said a

small prayer before looking inside. I hoped Ethel was in full view, because I really didn't want to go inside and search for her. I sucked in some air, stepped into the doorway, and froze. The double-wide was filled with raccoons. The raccoon closest to me was working on a jar of peanut butter. He opened his mouth and something fell out. It looked like a finger, but I'm going with hot dog. I backed out, turned, and hustled to my car.

"Was Ethel in there?" Lula asked. "How come you didn't close the door?"

"Raccoons."

"Say what?"

"It's filled with raccoons. They were eating cereal and stuff and rearranging the furniture."

"Did you see Ethel?"

"If Ethel was in the double-wide the raccoons wouldn't be there. Ethel would have those raccoons for lunch."

"You should get those raccoons to leave," Lula said. "They're gonna make a mess."

"They already made a mess, and I have no clue how to get them out. Stick a fork in me. I'm done here."

• • •

I dropped Lula off at the bonds office and called Joe Morelli. Morelli is a plainclothes cop in Trenton. He works crimes against persons. Mostly pulls homicides. And he's pretty much my boyfriend.

I've known Morelli just about all my life. Some of our times together have been good, and some have been not so good. Lately they've been comfortable. Past experience tells me that the comfort level could change in a heartbeat. He's six feet tall and slim with hard-toned muscle. His hair is black and wavy, and because he's on cop salary he always needs a cut. You put him in a suit and he looks like an Atlantic City casino pit boss. In jeans and a T-shirt he's totally hot. He has a big orange shaggy-haired dog named Bob, a serviceable green SUV, and a small house that he inherited from his Aunt Rose.

"Yo," Morelli said on the first ring.

"I have a problem."

"Me too," Morelli said. "I'm thinking about you naked, and you aren't here."

"You know Simon Diggery's snake, right?"

"Ethel."

"Yes. She's sort of escaped. Simon's in the lockup, and I think Ethel is slithering around the neighborhood."

"And?"

"And she's a fifty-pound boa! She might eat things that don't want to get eaten. Like cats and dogs and little people. She might even eat *big* people."

"I know that neighborhood. Ethel could only improve it."

"What if Ethel gets out of the neighborhood?"

"Cupcake, she's not going to get out of the neighborhood. Someone will spot her, and she'll be snake stew."

"I promised Simon I would take care of her."

I heard Morelli blow out a sigh, and I knew he was staring down at his shoe. Probably thinking he could have any woman

7

he wanted and wondering why he wanted me. I often wondered the same thing.

"Is this heading somewhere?" he asked.

"Yes, but I don't know where. In the interest of public safety, should people be notified that there's a boa wandering around looking for a snack?"

"The morally correct answer is *yes*, but the practical answer is *no*. Simon's neighborhood would be filled with snake hunters, four or five government agencies would want to take the snake away from him, and my sister-in-law, who hates snakes, would panic."

"I don't suppose you'd want to help me look for Ethel."

"Thought you'd never ask."

"I'll be at your house in ten minutes."

• • •

The sun was low in the sky when Morelli and I got to the dirt road leading to Simon's double-wide. Morelli drove at a crawl, and we peered out, looking for Ethel in the scrubby front yards of the locals. The road was about two miles long, partially wooded and partially cleared by squatters living in shacks, trailers, patched-together bungalows, and an occasional yurt. Abandoned cars served as chicken coops and guesthouses. Simon's place was at the end of the road.

Morelli parked in what served as Simon's driveway, and we got out and stood, hands on hips, taking it all in.

"Now what?" Morelli asked.

"I guess we should start with the double-wide. Maybe you could peek inside to see if Ethel came home."

"Me?"

"Yeah."

"Why me?"

"You're the big, strong cop. You've got a gun and muscles and stuff."

"What about you?"

"I'm the cupcake."

Morelli crossed the yard and looked inside the mobile home. "Whoa!"

"Raccoons?" I asked him.

Morelli backed out. "Cats. Everywhere. I swear there must be a hundred of them. And they don't look friendly. I think they're eating rats."

"So Ethel wasn't in there?"

"Just the cats and the rats."

"The cats must have gotten into the freezer. Simon kept a bag of frozen rats in case he couldn't find roadkill."

"More likely it was the raccoons that opened the freezer."

"Ethel can't have gone far," I said. "She doesn't move fast. Last I saw her she was halfway up the big oak tree on the edge of the property. Maybe you could track her. You could use your Boy Scout skills."

"I was never a Boy Scout," Morelli said. "I was the scourge of the neighborhood."

This was true. Morelli and his brothers bullied Boy Scouts and romanced Girl Scouts. Mothers all over Trenton warned their kids to stay far away from the Morelli boys. Not that the kids paid any attention. The Morelli boys were irresistible charmers.

"Huey, Dewey, and Louie were Junior Woodchucks," I said. "I always thought that was odd since they were actually ducks."

Morelli stared at me for a long moment. Probably wondering what the heck I was talking about since he'd only read superhero comics when he was a kid.

"She's a big fat snake," I said. "She has to have left some sort of trail."

"Suppose we find her. Then what?"

"I stopped at Giovichinni's before I came to your house, and I bought a couple packages of hot dogs. We can use them to lure Ethel back to Simon's double-wide."

That didn't exactly work when Simon tried it, but I couldn't come up with anything better. We crossed the yard and found some matted-down scrub grass that might have been a snake trail. We followed it into a patch of woods and pretended we knew what we were doing. The sun was setting, and it was increasingly dark in the woods. I had the flashlight app working on my cellphone, but visibility wasn't perfect, and I was terrified that I might inadvertently trip over Ethel.

"I can see light shining through the trees in front of us," Morelli said. "We must have crossed through the woods to Simon's neighbor's. I'm voting to bag the snake search for tonight."

"That would be my vote too. I'm not crazy about running into Ethel in the dark."

We continued out of the woods and stood staring at the run-down ranch house in front of us. It was about the size of a double-wide and looked like it was held together with duct tape and Elmer's glue. The rusted-out pickup truck in the front yard had double gun racks across the back window.

"Maybe we should ask if they've seen Ethel since we're here," I said to Morelli.

"Not a good idea. If they've seen her I can guarantee they're having her for dinner. If they haven't seen her, they'll comb the woods with their dogs until they find her."

"Okay then, how about if we creep up on them and peek in their kitchen window so we can see if they have the slow cooker going?"

"No. Another bad idea. The mayor frowns on cops moonlighting as peeping toms."

"Understood. So you stay here, and I'm going to take a quick look."

"No!"

Too late. I was halfway across the yard doing a tippy-toe jog. I got as far as the junker truck, and dogs started barking inside the house. The front door opened, and a man looked out. I held my breath and stood statue still. I was in shadow, behind the truck, and I was pretty sure he couldn't see me. The door slammed shut, and I could hear the man yelling at the dogs. The dogs kept barking, the door opened again, and the dogs charged out. Three of them. They were running straight for me, and I had a double fear. The first was that they would tear me to shreds. The second was that Morelli would shoot them.

I had one of the packages of wieners in my sweatshirt pocket. I tore the package open with my teeth and threw the hot dogs at the lead dog. He snapped up a wiener, and it turned into a feeding frenzy when the other dogs reached him and the remaining food.

Morelli ran across the yard, grabbed my sweatshirt sleeve, and yanked me toward the road. We reached the road and walked hand in hand back to the car.

"This was fun," Morelli said. "We should do this more often."

"Tomorrow?"

"No."

We were at the car, and we took a last look around. The sun had set, and the double-wide was a black blob in the darkness. There was some rustling in the surrounding brush, but aside from that it was quiet. No dogs barking. No cats howling. No one screaming that they were being eaten alive by a giant snake.

"Do you think we should look inside before we leave?" I asked Morelli.

"No," Morelli said. "We should definitely not look inside."

Forty-five minutes later Morelli pulled to the curb in front of his house.

"Usually Simon gets rebonded when he misses his date," Morelli said. "What's the deal with him staying in jail?"

"He's being stalked by zombies. He figures he's safer if he's locked up."

That got a smile out of Morelli. "One of the disadvantages to being a grave robber. I guess occasionally you dig up a zombie."

"He said he dug into a portal."

"That can't be good."

I cut my eyes to Morelli. "You don't believe in zombies, do you?"

"No. Do you?"

"No, of course not." And if I *did* believe in zombies I for sure wouldn't admit to it.

. . .

Bob did his happy dance when we walked through the door. His happiness was enhanced by the fact that we were carrying hot dogs. I snagged a couple bottles of beer from Morelli's fridge, and we all went out to the backyard. Morelli fired up the grill, and before long we were all stuffed full of hot dogs.

"So, what's new?" I asked Morelli.

Morelli cracked open a second beer. "Someone was decapitated last night. Male Caucasian without identification. He was found in the alley behind the hardware store on Broad Street. Looks like he was dragged there. The ME puts the time of death around four A.M."

"Is it your case?"

"Yeah, lucky me."

"And?"

"And I got nothing. I'm waiting for the lab reports to come back."

"You didn't recognize him?"

"No one recognized him. He didn't have a head."

"Are you serious?"

"Unfortunately, yes. No head. Gone without a trace. We checked all the dumpsters in the area but nada."

My job was bad enough. If I had Morelli's job I'd be a raging alcoholic. Every day he was, figuratively speaking, ankle deep in blood. He witnessed scenes of horrible crimes committed by sick people. And despite this, for the most part he could sleep at night, and he hadn't lost faith in the human race. He'd become a master at compartmentalizing. I'm not so good at it. I frequently sleep with the bedroom light on.

Morelli shut the grill down and wrapped an arm around me. "You know what comes next?"

"Ice cream?"

"I haven't got any ice cream."

"What *do* you have?"

Morelli grinned. "Something better than ice cream."

"Hard to believe."

"The key word is *hard*."

Oh boy.

TWO

MORELLI LIVES IN a neighborhood of good people packed into modest houses on minimal lots. His front yard is plain. His grass is kept neat. No flowers. No shrubs. No plastic pink flamingos or plaster statues of the Virgin Mary. He has a large flat-screen television in his living room, a pool table in his dining room, and a small table with two chairs in his kitchen. There are three small bedrooms and a full bath upstairs. The master has a king-size bed, which is a good thing because Bob takes up a lot of space.

Morelli is an early riser, always eager to start his day. On the rare occasion he's not completely eager, he's still propelled forward by routine. My routine has a slower start. I'm mostly *reluctant* to start my day. Especially when it involves looking for a snake.

Sunlight was pouring into Morelli's room by the time I

dragged myself out of his bed and into the shower. We didn't cohabitate, but I spent enough time there to warrant space in the closet. I retrieved some clean clothes, got dressed, went downstairs, and let Bob out to roam around the backyard. I toasted a bagel, helped myself to coffee, and talked myself into heading out to the office.

. . .

Vincent Plum Bail Bonds is housed in a small storefront office on Hamilton Avenue. It's between the hospital and the bakery, and it's across the street from Chambersburg, better known as the Burg. I grew up in the Burg, and my parents still live there. When I was a kid, the Burg was predominantly Italian with some eastern Europeans scattered here and there. It was home to mostly midlevel mob families and second-generation Americans. The population is more diverse now, but it's still a neighborhood that has strong family bonds, keeps itself clean, and takes pride in displaying the flag.

Lula was already at the office when I rolled in.

"Look at you," Lula said. "I can tell you got some last night. You got that satisfied look on you."

It was true that I got some. And it was true that it was satisfying, but that was last night, and I thought the satisfaction Lula was seeing this morning was more from the bagel.

"What's new?" I asked Connie. "Did any skips come in this morning?"

Connie is the office manager. She's a couple years older than me, she's twice as Italian, and if she was in a bitch-slapping contest with the Rock, my money would be on her.

"We have two new high bonds," Connie said, sliding the files across her desk.

I paged through the files and gave Lula the condensed version. "Edward Koot. Fifty-seven years old. Shot up a coffeehouse because he said they shorted him on his caramel macchiato. Went outside in a rage and shot up four cars before he was knocked out by a senior citizen who smacked him with a HurryCane. No one was injured except Koot. He had a concussion and got a bunch of stitches in the back of his head."

"You don't want to mess with them HurryCanes," Lula said. "They're built to last. I got a neighbor has one of them. Koot got any priors?"

"He was put in an anger management program after a road rage incident."

"Guess we know how that worked out," Lula said.

"The second FTA is Zero Slick," I said.

"I like him already," Lula said. "That's an awesome name."

"He's twenty-nine years old, five feet two inches, and he lists his gender as 'questionable.'"

"Guess that covers all the bases," Lula said. "He must be a confused individual. What'd he do?"

"He accidentally blew up an apartment building on State Street."

"That don't sound so bad," Lula said. "It was a accident, right?"

"He was cooking a massive batch of meth at the time."

17

"Everybody knows it's best you do that in *small* batches," Lula said. "He should have read the instructions. He's lucky he didn't die."

"It says here that he was out smoking weed when the meth blew."

"Now that I'm thinking about it, I remember seeing this on the news. There wasn't nothing left of that building. Not that it mattered much on account of it was empty except for the meth cooker. It was gonna be torn down."

"There's more," Connie said. "He also left the scene in one of the fire trucks and ran over two police cars before driving through the front door of a 7-Eleven. Rumor has it he's suing the city for discrimination because the fire truck wasn't equipped for a five-foot two-inch truck jacker to drive safely."

"I always wanted to drive a fire truck," Lula said. "I might think about being a fireman except they gotta wear them man shoes, and it would ruin my look. I got a image to protect."

Lula's image for the day involved a bursting-at-the-seams, super-short blue metallic bandage dress that matched her hair, and silver sandals with a three-inch wedge. If I tried to wear something like that I'd look like an idiot, but it seemed to work for Lula. I suppose it's all about expectations.

"I've done preliminary phone work on Koot and Slick," Connie said. "They don't appear to be employed. Koot got fired from his job as a security guard when he shot up the coffeehouse. Slick lists his occupation as 'pharmaceutical activist.' High school graduate. No work history. He's bounced around the country. Seattle, Chicago, Denver."

"And now he's here," Lula said. "Lucky us."

"His parents live in Hamilton Township," Connie said. "I spoke to his mother on the phone, and she said she didn't know where he was staying, but she might be a place for you to start anyway."

"He's probably on the lookout for another abandoned building," Lula said. "I'm suggesting we get a list of them and go trolling. I want to see what someone named Zero Slick looks like."

"We have a photo," I said. "He doesn't look like much. Chubby guy with brown ponytail."

Lula glanced at the photo. "I was hoping for something better. Like he should have some tattoos or purple hair. This man doesn't look like he's living up to his name."

"Maybe he's more Zero Slick in person," I said. "We can hunt him down as soon as we check on Ethel."

Lula's eyes got wide. "Ethel? You mean you haven't found Ethel yet? No way am I going searching for Ethel. Look at me. Do I look like I'm dressed for a snake jamboree? I don't think so."

"You can wait in the car."

"I guess I could do that, but don't expect me to get out and go traipsing around."

"Fine. Great. Wait in the car."

"You sound like you're all upset about this," Lula said.

"If you wore more sensible clothes and shoes, you would be able to do more traipsing."

"If I wore rubber boots up to my pussy I still wouldn't go look in that double-wide," Lula said.

Connie glanced over at me. "She has a point."

I blew out a sigh and hiked my messenger bag higher on my shoulder. I said adios to Connie and left the office.

"Your car or mine?" I asked Lula.

"Your car. I just had mine detailed, and I'm not driving my baby on Diggery's dirt road."

My "baby" did just fine on Diggery's dirt road, because my SUV was a POS that looked like it hadn't been detailed in ten years. I wasn't even sure of the paint color under the grime.

We saw no sign of Ethel on the way in and no sign of Ethel when I parked in front of the double-wide. It was morning, and all was quiet in Diggery's neighborhood. I left Lula in the car and carefully walked to the makeshift steps and open door. It was eerily still. No snorting, slurping animal sounds. No sound of an elephant crashing into furniture. I crept to the top step and looked in. It wasn't as bad as I'd feared. Cabinet doors were open, cereal boxes and jelly jars were scattered around, an upholstered chair had been ripped apart. For all I know the chair might have looked like that when Diggery was in residence. The double-wide didn't smell all that great, but again, it never smelled good. I didn't see Ethel.

"Hello," I called. "Anybody home?"

No answer.

The bedroom and bathroom doors were open. I suppose Ethel could have been curled up snoozing in one of those rooms. I wasn't about to investigate. Doorstep was as far as I was willing to go.

I got halfway across the yard, on my way back to my SUV,

and I stopped. This was stupid. I went into filthy, dark, rat-infested buildings looking for rapists and murderers, but I was chickening out on Diggery's double-wide. I blew out a sigh, rolled my eyes, turned, and marched up to the door and stepped in. Not so bad, I told myself. No raccoons, no cats, no rats, dead or otherwise, no snakes in sight. I made my way to the back bedroom and took a quick look around. No Ethel anywhere. I left the double-wide and returned to Lula.

"Well?" Lula asked.

"Empty."

"Good," Lula said. "Let's roll. I'm feeling creeped out. I think there's zombies around here somewhere. I could feel them watching me. Probably the only reason there's no cats left in that crap-ass double-wide is on account of the zombies scared them off."

"I thought zombies only came out at night."

"No way. That's vampires. Zombies never sleep. Okay, so they like the dark, but I'm guessing they could use sunscreen and be okay. The thing is at night they're the most dangerous because that's when they get hungry and want to eat brains."

"Good to know."

"You bet your ass. You gotta be real careful of zombies at night."

I put the car in gear and headed out of Diggery's neighborhood. "What's the address on Slick's file?" I asked Lula.

"He hasn't got an address. Probably he's living under the bridge."

"Did Connie give us his parents' address?"

"They're in that big apartment complex by the senior citizen place. Unit 106."

I took Hamilton to Klockner and turned off Klockner into Majestic Mews Apartments. I rolled through the maze of two-story garden apartment buildings, finally locating 106. It was a ground-floor unit with a pot of fake yellow mums at the front door. Very cheery.

"Who we gonna be this time?" Lula asked. "How about if we're Girl Scouts selling cookies? We haven't done that one in a long time."

I parked in the lot in front of the apartment. "How about if we're bond enforcement and politely ask a few questions?"

"That never works. No one likes us when we're bond enforcement."

I got out of the car, hung my bag on my shoulder, walked to the door, and rang the bell. A motherly looking woman in her fifties answered.

"Mrs. Slick?" I asked.

"Goodness, no," she said. "I'm Mrs. Krakowski."

I introduced myself and told her I was looking for Zero Slick.

A man came up behind the woman. "Who is it?" he asked.

"She's looking for Zero Slick," the woman said.

The man squinted at me. "Are you a prostitute?"

"No," I said. "I work for Vincent Plum Bail Bonds."

Lula leaned forward. "You got something against prostitutes?"

I stepped in front of Lula. "I was given this address for Zero Slick's parents."

"That's us," the man said. "Our name wasn't good enough for him. He had to make something up."

"He's very creative," the woman said. "He's always been a free spirit."

"Free spirit my ass," the man said. "He's a damn snowflake. I didn't even know what a snowflake was until I heard it on the news, and here I am . . . I got one."

"Snowflakes are beautiful," the woman said. "Each one is unique."

"For crissake, Marie," the man said. "Give it up. He's twenty-nine years old, and he's never had a job. He doesn't even know if he's a boy or a girl. What's with that? I changed his diaper. I guess I know what he is."

"It's complicated," Marie said.

"It's not complicated. If it hangs outside you're a boy."

"I think he's making a social statement," Marie said. "He's at the forefront of human rights."

"I'd like him to be at the forefront of getting a job. How long am I going to have to support this freeloader?"

"You don't support him," Marie said.

"I know you give him money," the man said. "I'm working double shifts at the plant, and you've got a food budget that would feed forty people. Where's all that food go to?"

"Does he live here?" I asked.

"No," Marie said. "You know these young people. They like to be independent."

"Do you have an address for him?"

"Of course," Marie said. "He lives in an apartment building in town."

"He doesn't live there," the man said. "He blew it the fuck up."

"You know I don't like that word," Marie said to her husband.

"He's a drug addict," the man said. "He smokes dope."

Marie leaned forward and whispered to Lula and me. "He's really a good boy at heart."

I gave Marie my card. "If you get an address for him I'd appreciate a call."

"Of course," Marie said.

"You gotta respect a mother like that," Lula said on the way back to the car. "It was real touching the way she always found something nice to say about her loser kid."

"He was peddling meth. There must be people on the street who know where to find him."

"He was trying to cook some," Lula said. "It's not clear if he ever sold any."

"Okay, so we know he smokes weed. He has to buy that from someone."

"Weed's everywhere," Lula said. "You get the special of the day from Cluck-in-a-Bucket and it comes with a side of weed."

I looked over at Lula and raised my eyebrows.

"Only when Clarence is working the drive-thru window," Lula said.

"Read through his file. Does he have a significant other? He's some sort of activist. Does he belong to any organizations? Political affiliation?"

"There's nothing like that in here."

I called Morelli. "I'm looking for a twenty-nine-year-old guy who has no job and no address. He's confused about his gender, and he blew up a building trying to cook meth."

"Zero Slick," Morelli said.

"Yeah. How do I find him?"

"He's a paid activist. He gets fifty bucks and a ride on a bus, and he holds up a sign at whatever event he's assigned."

"And?"

"Don't know beyond that. You need to look for some sort of protest."

I disconnected and drove out of the lot. "You need to find a protest," I said to Lula.

"Anything special you have in mind?"

"No."

"How am I supposed to do this?"

"Go to Google and ask for future protests in Jersey."

"Google isn't telling me anything," Lula said, "but there's some idiot holding a town hall fiasco at the firehouse tonight. I know about it on account of they canceled bingo. Your granny is probably going to be there protesting the canceling. Does that count?"

My Grandma Mazur moved in with my parents when my grandfather checked in to Hotel Heaven. My father is of the opinion that this left him in hell on earth. My mother is a good Catholic woman who goes to mass at least three times a week and prays for God to help her have a cheerful, charitable attitude. When that doesn't work, she drinks. Personally, I think Grandma is a hoot, but then I don't have to live with her.

"Do you know anything about the idiot?" I asked Lula.

"He's some politician."

"Good enough. Do you want to go to a town hall fiasco with me tonight?"

"Sure. Haven't got anything better to do since they canceled bingo."

THREE

EDWARD KOOT WAS next on my to-do list. He lived alone in a small row house three blocks from the coffee house he shot up. I thought chances were good that he was home since he was now unemployed.

"He even looks angry in his picture," Lula said, paging through Koot's file. "I could tell you what his problem is right now. He needs Botox. I always say, you are what you look. I bet you shoot this man up with Botox, and his whole personality changes."

I slowly drove past Koot's house. No activity on the street. Shades drawn on all the windows. I turned into the alley that intersected the block and stopped when I got to the back of his house.

"Someone's in there," Lula said. "The shade's up, and I can see someone walking past the window. Probably it's the kitchen."

I dropped Lula off with instructions to stay put unless he bolted. I drove around to the front, parked, and went to the front door.

Koot answered on my second knock. "What?" he asked.

I introduced myself and told him he'd missed a court date and needed to reschedule.

"I'm not going to no stupid kangaroo court," Koot said. "I'm the one who should be suing. Every day I get a caramel macchiato. I'm a loyal paying customer. And all of a sudden I get a half a macchiato from some new little snip just started working there. And do you know what she told me when I asked for the rest of my macchiato? She said, 'Move along, old man. You're holding up the line.' The hell I will, I told her. And then she said she was gonna call the police. Can you imagine? It was like I was on an airplane. What's happening to this country?"

"I understand your frustration, but probably it wasn't a good idea to shoot up the coffee shop."

"You can only push a man so far," Koot said.

"You left the coffee shop and took out four innocent cars."

"I admit I got carried away. It was like I was in a frenzy, but I wouldn't have gotten all frenzied up if I'd had my macchiato. It's a calming influence in the morning. It starts my day off with a smile."

"Did you have a macchiato today?"

"Yeah. I go to Starbucks now. It's a longer walk, but they care about their coffee. I get a full cup. Right up to the top. Every time. And it's nice and hot but not too hot."

My phone rang, and I saw that it was Lula.

"What's going on?" she asked.

"We're talking."

"Just checking. Wanted to make sure you didn't leave without me."

I disconnected and turned my attention back to Koot. "Here's the thing," I said. "You need to come with me and get rebonded."

"No. Not going to happen. None of this was my fault. End of story."

He attempted to close the door, but I had my foot in it.

"You'll have a chance to tell all this to the judge," I said.

"Get your foot out of my door, or I'll shoot it."

"Have you ever thought about Botox for that wrinkle in your forehead?" I asked.

"Wrinkle? What?"

"You have a big wrinkle between your eyes, and it makes you look angry."

"That's because I *am* angry. You're disturbing my day. And I don't like you."

He wrenched the door open, gave me a shove with both hands, and I stumbled back. He slammed the door shut and by the time I got it open, he was running toward the back of the house. I charged after him and saw him exit through the kitchen. I heard him shriek, and then all was quiet. I looked out the back door and saw that Koot was facedown and Lula was sitting on him.

"Is he breathing?" I asked her.

"Hard to tell."

I cuffed him, Lula got off, and I pulled him to his feet.

29

"Are you going to read me my rights?" he asked.

"I'm a bounty hunter," I said. "You haven't got any rights. You signed them all away when you took out the bail bond."

We loaded Koot into my SUV and drove him to the police station. I turned him in and picked up my body receipt.

"That was easy," Lula said. "We got our A game on today. We got good juju. I can't wait to rumble at the rally tonight."

"We aren't going to rumble. We're going to quietly stand at the back of the room and try to spot Slick."

"Sure, I know that, but we might have to rumble a little if things get dicey."

. . .

I dropped Lula off at the office and went to my parents' house to mooch lunch. They live five minutes from the office, five minutes from Morelli's house, and a time warp away from me. Even when my mom gets a new refrigerator or buys new curtains the house still feels precisely the same as when I was in school. It's equally comforting and disturbing.

The duplex is small, and cluttered, and immaculately clean. Living room, dining room, kitchen on the first floor. Three small bedrooms and a bathroom on the second floor. My father is seldom home for lunch. He's retired from the post office, but he drives a cab part-time.

I parked on the street, and by the time I got to the front door Grandma Mazur already had it open.

"Just in time for lunch," she said. "We have olive loaf from Giovichinni's, and Italian cookies from the bakery."

I followed Grandma to the kitchen at the back of the house and took a chair at the little wooden table. I ate breakfast and lunch at the same table when I was a kid. After school I did my homework there.

"We got company for lunch," Grandma said to my mom.

My mom was pulling food out of the fridge. Pickles, mustard, macaroni salad, cold cuts, a loaf of bread. "Is olive loaf okay?" she asked me.

"Olive loaf is great," I said.

My mom is the anchor in the family. She represents normal . . . at least what's considered normal in the Burg. Grandma and I have totally gone rogue.

Grandma set out plates, knives, forks, water glasses. "Did you hear, some idiot politician is talking at the firehouse tonight," she said. "So, they canceled bingo. I don't know what this neighborhood's coming to. You can't count on anything anymore." She sat down and spooned some macaroni salad onto her plate. "Last night I went to pay my respects to Leonard Friedman, and they had a closed casket. It shouldn't be allowed. There should be a law. If you go to see someone one last time you should be able to *see* them."

"He didn't have a head," my mother said.

"I admit, that makes it tricky, but they could have gotten around it somehow," Grandma said. "Maybe they should have made more of an effort to *find* his head in the first place."

"Was he the man killed behind the hardware store?" I asked.

"No," Grandma said. "Lenny passed at home. Heart attack. A big one. He lost his head at the mortuary. I'm told he was slid into the meat locker on arrival and when they pulled him out next morning he didn't have a head." Grandma made herself a sandwich with olive loaf and Swiss cheese. "Emily Molinowski was in the drawer next to Lenny, and I guess she lost her head too. I'm glad I'm not dead this week. When I have my viewing I want to have my head. And I want Evelyn Stoddard to do my makeup. She has a good touch. Sometimes Julie Gross does makeup at Stiva's, and I'm not a fan of her lipstick selections."

Stiva's funeral parlor is a social center for Grandma and her lady friends. It's free entertainment. It's available seven days a week. And you can count on cookies being served in the lobby.

In the past, Grandma has been known to pry open a closed casket, unlocking it with her nail file, so she could take a peek. On these occasions my mother bypasses prayer and goes straight for the Jim Beam.

"Let me get this straight," I said to Grandma. "Someone severed two heads at Stiva's, and the heads haven't been found?"

"Yep," Grandma said. "Pass the pickles to me."

"How could that happen?"

"I guess it happened at night," Grandma said. "They came in first thing in the morning to do the embalming, pulled out the trays, and no heads."

"Wasn't everything locked up? Doesn't Stiva's have a security system? Didn't an alarm go off?"

"Yes. Yes. And no," Grandma said. "People are thinking it must be an inside job, but I've got another theory. I think it was the zombies. There's rumors going around that there've been zombie sightings. And you know how they like to eat brains. Well, you put two and two together and it makes sense."

My mother very carefully spread mustard across a slice of bread and precisely placed olive loaf and Swiss cheese onto the mustard. I suspected she was making an effort to stay calm when what she really wanted to do was shake Grandma until her false teeth flew out of her mouth and she stopped rambling on about zombies.

Grandma forked up some macaroni, and I spotted a ring on her finger.

"Is that a new ring?" I asked her.

"It's a friendship ring," Grandma said. "I got a boyfriend. He's a pip."

My mother gave up a sigh and cut her sandwich into halves.

"Do I know him?" I asked.

"I met him on one of those Internet sites," Grandma said. "He lives in Florida. By Key West. I might go down there to visit him. He's a real hottie."

I sneaked a look at my mom, but she wasn't making eye contact. She was staring at her sandwich.

"What does he do?" I asked Grandma.

"Mostly he fishes. He was a dockworker in Newark, but he's retired now."

"Not married?"

"His wife died a while back. He has kids but they're in Jersey."

"You have to be careful about Internet connections," I said. "You never really know who you're talking to."

"He could be a serial killer," my mother said. "He could be a terrorist. He could be some pervert sex fiend."

"He might be too old to be a sex fiend," Grandma said, "but I guess he could be a killer."

"Why me?" my mother asked.

"Don't send him any money," I said to Grandma. "And don't go to Florida."

"He could be the one," Grandma said, pulling up a photo on her phone, handing the phone over to me.

"This is George Hamilton," I said.

Grandma took the phone back and studied the photo. "He does look a little like George Hamilton, but my honey's name is Roger Murf. Him and George are handsome devils, aren't they?"

From the corner of my eye I saw my mom shaking her head and making the sign of the cross. Next stop would be a trip to the liquor cabinet over the sink.

"Did you send him a picture of you?" I asked Grandma.

"Sort of," Grandma said. "I didn't have a real good picture, so I sent him one of your mother. We look alike except for the hair, and I'm thinking about going brown anyway."

My mother sucked in some air and her eyes went wide. "You didn't! Tell me you didn't!"

"It was a nice picture," Grandma said. "It was the one where you're on the beach at Seaside."

My mother did the sign of the cross again. "Holy Mother," she said.

I had a second helping of macaroni, finished my sandwich, ate a bunch of Italian cookies, and pushed my chair back from the table.

"Gotta go," I said. "Things to do."

"Are you hunting down bad guys?" Grandma asked.

"Eventually."

I gave hugs to Grandma and my mom, thanked them for lunch, and escaped to my car. I stopped at the supermarket on the way home and got a couple more packages of hot dogs for Ethel, Pop-Tarts for my hamster Rex and me, bread, cereal, bananas, and assorted frozen dinner–type foods.

FOUR

IT WAS CLOSE to three o'clock when I lugged my groceries into my apartment building and down the hall to my place. I put the key in the lock, pushed the door open, and yelped. There was a man in my place.

He was over six feet tall, broad shouldered, slim hipped, and nicely muscled. He was beach-bum tan with thick, unruly blond hair cut short, and dark eyebrows and eyelashes that I would kill to have. He was wearing jeans with a rip in the knee, a T-shirt that advertised tequila, and black-and-white sneaker-type shoes. He was drop-dead handsome with perfect white teeth and a lot of attitude. I know about the attitude because I know the man. His name is Diesel. That's it. Just Diesel.

He dropped into my life for the first time several years ago at Christmas, scaring the heck out of me when he suddenly appeared in my kitchen. When I'd asked him how he'd gotten into my apartment and my life, he said, "Sweetcakes, you wouldn't believe me if I told you." Nothing much has changed since then.

He's visited a bunch of times since that Christmas, mysteriously coming and going. He doesn't have a key to my apartment, but that never stops him from getting in.

"Surprise," Diesel said.

"Now what?" I asked him.

"Just passing through and thought I'd say hello."

He took a grocery bag from me, set it on the counter, and emptied it.

"There are these things called vegetables," he said. "You ever hear about them?"

"If I want vegetables I eat at my parents' house. And I have baby carrots in the fridge."

"They're for your rat."

"He's a *hamster*."

Diesel opened the box of Frosted Flakes and took a handful.

"You never just stop in to say hello," I said. "I haven't seen or heard from you in over a year. What's up?"

"There's a disturbance in the force. Thought I'd check it out."

"That's a little vague."

Diesel shrugged. "It's what I do, sweetie pie."

"Right. You weren't planning on doing it here, were you? Like in my apartment?"

"I'd rather be under a palm tree somewhere, but yeah, I'm stuck here for a while."

"No. You are *not* staying here."

"Sure I am. I always stay here. You'd be heartbroken if I stayed somewhere else."

"I'd be overjoyed."

"You need to work on your hostess skills," Diesel said. "The whole cranky thing is a major turnoff."

"Morelli is coming over for dinner tonight. I don't want you here when he walks in."

"Honey, that's hard to believe. No one would come here for dinner. You only own one pot."

"I own several pots and a fry pan."

Diesel grinned. "You're going to give him that frozen mac and cheese, aren't you?"

"The mac and cheese is for me. Morelli is bringing dinner."

"Okay, I'm in."

"You aren't in. There's no *in* for you. He's bringing dinner, and he's spending the night."

"You need to change that plan. I'm not crazy about sharing a bed with Morelli."

I'd been down this road before with Diesel. He was an immovable object. Too big and strong to push around. Too intelligent to out-psych. He was inexplicably likable, and he smelled like fresh-out-of-the-oven gingerbread. He also left as abruptly and as easily as he appeared. He was an okay guy to know, but a romantic attachment would be a disaster.

"Okay. Great. You can have my apartment, and I'll temporarily move in with Morelli," I said.

"Not gonna happen," Diesel said.

"How do you know?"

"Spidey sense."

I put my groceries away, gave Rex a small piece of Pop-Tart, and went into my bedroom, where I found Diesel sprawled across my bed.

"What are you doing?" I asked him.

"Thinking. Want to join me?"

"No."

"Afraid you might like it?"

"Yes."

That got another grin out of him. He reached for me and I ran away, back to the kitchen. I ate what was left of the Pop-Tart, and I called Morelli.

"Yo," he said. "I was just about to call you. I'm going to have to cancel dinner tonight. We've got a situation here."

"I've got a situation too. What's your situation?"

"We found some heads."

"The ones without bodies?"

"Yeah. Problem is we've got more heads than bodies now."

"How many heads do you have?"

"I'm not authorized to say, but it's more than three and less than ten."

"That could be a lot of heads."

"Actually, it's less than five," Morelli said.

"Have they been identified?"

"Three have been identified."

"What about the headless guy found behind the hardware store?"

"It looks like one of the heads might belong to him, but the circumstances are odd. The autopsy has him dying from a heart attack several hours before his head was removed."

"Eeuuww."

"Exactly. It's like someone has a head fetish. I'm really tied up here. It would be great if you could walk Bob for me, and maybe we could have a late dinner."

"No problem."

I disconnected and marched back to the bedroom.

"So much for Spidey sense," I said to Diesel.

"Honeypot, you don't ever want to underestimate my Spidey sense."

"Here's the plan. I'm leaving. I'm going to look for a snake and an FTA. Then I'm going to Morelli's house. I'd appreciate it if you'd talk to Rex once in a while. Make sure he has fresh water. And don't eat all the mac and cheese."

I threw some clothes and a package of hot dogs into a small duffel bag, said goodbye to Rex, and told him I'd be back. I left the apartment and headed for my car. Truth is I wasn't crazy about the whole leaving thing, but I didn't know what else to do. I was involved in a relationship with Morelli, and he wouldn't be happy to hear I was cohabitating with Diesel.

· · ·

I drove to Diggery's double-wide, parked, and peeked inside. No cats. No raccoons. No rats. No snake. Horrible smell. I didn't spend a lot of time peeking. I jumped into my car and looked for Ethel as I inched my way along the road and out of the neighborhood. No luck.

Next stop was Morelli's house. I opened the front door and heard Bob galloping at me from the kitchen. I braced myself, but he still knocked me back against the wall and gave me a lot of Bob kisses. I told him he was a good boy and thanked him for the kisses and he seemed happy with that. I hooked him up to his leash and walked him around several blocks. He pooped twice, and I didn't pick it up. My feeling is if God wanted me to pick up dog poop he would have made it look like diamonds and smell like roses.

I fed Bob and helped myself to a frozen waffle. I was paging through my emails when I got a text from Lula saying she needed a ride, and she saw on the news that protesters were already collecting at the firehouse. Twenty minutes later I had Lula in my car, and I was driving back toward the Burg.

"Is something wrong with your car?" I asked her.

"No. My baby's just fine, but I wasn't gonna take it into no protest zone. Someone throws rocks at *your* car and turns it over wheels up, it's no loss. I mean, sure it's your transportation, but it's not a classic like mine, right? I got a red Firebird. You don't never want anybody throwing rocks at a red Firebird. And it's got a custom sound system. That hummer'll shake the fillings out of your teeth when I crank it up. It's got bass, you see what I'm saying?"

I cut my eyes to her. "Next time you drive."

"Yeah, I'll do that. What do you think of my outfit? We might get to be on television if this thing gets out of hand, so I want to look good. I hear you shouldn't wear stuff with too much pattern, and that's why I went with this solid purple tank top."

41

Lula was wearing five-inch platform stilettos, a skirt that barely covered her ass, and a purple sequined tank top that was two sizes too small for her watermelon-size breasts.

"I like the tank top," I said. "Lots of sparkle."

"It's from my Vegas collection from when I was a 'ho. I got a lot of action when I wore this top. 'Course some of that was on account of I had a good corner back then."

I got a block away from the firehouse and passed two buses that were parked on the street.

"They're the protester buses," Lula said. "They bring in the professional protesters just in case there's not enough locals. It's just like Morelli said. And I read an article about this, too. I'm pretty sure you could get a degree in protesting if you go to the right college. It's a big thing now."

"I don't think there's a degree in protesting."

"There's a lot to learn," Lula said. "You gotta know about making signs and holding them up in the right fashion. And there's ways to be obnoxious and provoke a fight. Then you gotta shout slogans and such."

There were about sixty people milling around in front of the firehouse. They looked peaceful enough, holding signs, taking selfies on their smartphones. A bunch of uniformed cops stood on the perimeter. No riot gear. No nervous pacing. No guns drawn. Looking like they'd rather be someplace else.

"This here's disappointing," Lula said. "I expected some nastiness."

I parked a block away, and we walked back to the firehouse.

"Remember, we're here to tag Zero Slick. We're not getting involved in the protest."

"Nothing to get involved in," Lula said. "This is a yawn. And I don't get these signs some of them are holding. They say 'Hell, no, we won't go!' What's that mean, anyway?"

"I think they're left over from the sixties when people were protesting the Vietnam War," I said. "Someone probably grabbed the wrong signs from the warehouse."

"Hey," Lula said. "Look over by the street light. It's your granny and two other old ladies. And they got signs." Lula waved at Grandma. "Yoo-hoo! Granny!"

Grandma turned and saw us and waved her sign. It said BINGO MATTERS.

"Now, that's a good sign," Lula said. "It makes a real statement."

We didn't see Slick outside, so we went into the firehouse and stood to the back of the meeting room. There was a podium and an American flag at the far end, and rows of folding chairs had been set up for the audience. The room could probably accommodate seventy to eighty people if you squashed them in, but so far there were only fifteen people there.

"We must be early," Lula said.

I checked my watch. "Nope. We're right on time."

A woman came out and introduced the speaker. He was a nice-looking man in a blue suit. Glasses. Sandy blond hair. In his fifties.

Lula leaned forward. "Who did she say this guy was? I didn't catch it."

43

"He's running for some sort of council seat to replace a man who died."

The candidate at the podium started to speak, and all the protesters filed in from outside.

"I see him!" Lula said. "I'd know him anywhere."

"Slick?"

"No. The television guy. The one with the greased-up hair and the fake tan. And he's got a camera guy with him. Do I look okay? This could be my big chance. Is my hair okay?"

Lula was wearing her blond Farrah Fawcett wig. I was guessing it was also from the Vegas 'ho collection. On anyone else the whole deal would look ridiculous, but it was oddly spectacular on Lula.

"The hair's good," I said.

"It shows off my beautiful mahogany complexion," Lula said. This was true.

The problem with trying to find a five-two man in a crowd is that he doesn't stand out. It would be easier to spot Slick if he was six-five. I went seat by seat, row by row, trying to see around the signs. The protesters shouted at the poor man at the podium, and Grandma and her friends contributed to the chaos by chanting "We want bingo! We want bingo!"

"I'm getting a headache," Lula said. "The only people here who make any sense are your granny and her lady friends."

A woman carrying a HELL, NO sign tried to shove Lula out of the way so she could get to the front, and Lula planted her stiletto heel into the woman's foot.

"I'm injured," the woman shrieked. "This fat bitch broke my foot."

Lula leaned in and narrowed her eyes at the woman. "Say what?"

"Fat bitch," the woman said. "Fat 'ho bitch."

Lula reached for her purse, and I grabbed her arm. "Do *not* shoot her," I said. "I'll be really pissed off if you shoot her."

"How about if I just shoot her in the knee?"

"No!"

"Okay then, can I punch her in the face?"

"No."

Grandma was at my side. "What's going on? You need some muscle? I got my girls with me."

"Nothing's going on," I said.

People were collecting around us, there was a lot of jostling, and voices were raised. I saw the television guy moving in our direction.

"We need to get out of here," I said to Lula.

"I'm on it," Lula said. "Stick close."

I grabbed Grandma's wrist and tugged her after me. An object flew past and hit Lula in the back of the head. It exploded on impact and gushed red. My first thought was bomb. My second was tomato. I turned to look behind me and took a raw egg to the forehead.

The entire room had broken out into a free-for-all. The police rushed in and set off a flash grenade. People were screaming and trampling one another to get to the door. Lula detoured into the firehouse kitchen, and I followed her, dragging Grandma and the ladies along with us. We exited through the back door into an alley. Grandma and the ladies ditched their signs, and we crept around the building and looked out at the street. The protesters were clustered in front of the lone television guy and his cameraman. They still looked angry, gesturing at the police who were mostly stoic, clearing the way so the buses could get through to pick up their passengers.

I recognized one of the cops and sidled up to him. "Will you make any arrests?"

He shook his head no. "This is the Camden group. They're okay. They're just out here making some pizza money. We'll load them onto the buses, they'll stop at White Castle for burgers, and they'll be home before the ten o'clock news comes on."

"What about the man who was speaking?"

"He'll get elected," the cop said. "He's the only one running."

"I was hoping Zero Slick would be here. He's FTA, and I know he's an activist."

"He's probably protesting the Korean grocery on Madison and State. I heard that gig was assigned to the locals. We'll be heading over there as soon as we get these folks settled into their buses."

"Aren't you afraid there'll be trouble before you get there?"

"The television guy is still here. No one's going to act out on Madison until the television guy gets over there." He made a small grimace. "You know you've got egg on you, right?"

FIVE

LULA AND I took Grandma home and then we went to the Korean grocery on Madison. A handful of people were standing in front of the store, blocking the entrance. They were holding signs that called for DIVERSITY NOW.

I parked and approached one of the sign holders. "What's the problem?" I asked.

"Discriminatory hiring practices," he said.

"This store is owned by the Park family," Lula said. "I shop here all the time. They're real nice people. The whole family works here."

"Their hiring practices aren't sympathetic to diversity," the man said.

"That's because they're all Korean, you moron," Lula said. "This here's a family-run store. You see the sign over the door? It says 'Park Korean Grocery.' You know how many Parks there are? About forty. And they all live in two rooms over the store. What are all those people supposed to do if they can't dribble down into the store to stack vegetables?"

"They're fascists," the man said.

"You don't even know what that means," Lula said. "Go ahead and tell me what makes up a fascist."

I pulled Lula away. "We're supposed to be looking for Zero Slick, not inciting another riot."

"Well, I don't see no chubby short guy with a brown ponytail here. The only short person I see with a brown ponytail is an unattractive woman wearing a dress that's totally wrong for her. And she's wearing it with sneakers."

I located the woman. "That's Slick," I said.

"Well, he got no fashion sense. It's like he's giving women a bad name being dressed like that."

I had cuffs in the back pocket of my jeans and pepper spray hooked to my waistband. I also had a stun gun in my bag, but it was illegal so I preferred not to use it when there were witnesses. I walked around the group of protesters and came up behind Slick.

"Zero Slick?" I asked.

He turned and looked at me. "Yes?"

"I represent your bail bonds agent. You need to come with me to reschedule your court date."

"Sure," Slick said. "I'll have my social secretary get in touch with you."

I clapped a bracelet onto his wrist. "We need to do this now."

He yanked his arm away, but I held firm to the second cuff.

"Are you freaking nuts?" he said. "Can't you see I'm working? Get this thing off me."

I reached around to secure his other wrist, and he smacked me with his sign.

"Help!" he yelled. "Police brutality."

"I'm not a police officer," I said to him.

He waved his sign. *"Pig! Pig!"*

"You stop that," Lula said to him. "I don't like your attitude. And on top of that I'm offended by your accessorizing."

Word went out that the television guy had arrived, and in seconds we were surrounded by protesters demanding that I release Slick. Voices were raised. Someone shoved Lula, and she took him out with an elbow to the gut. After that it was bloody chaos. There was a flash and a *BANG!* And everyone stopped punching and eye gouging and stepped back.

"This is getting old," Lula said. "My ears are ringing. I better not have permanent damage."

I thought if the sound system in her car hadn't permanently damaged her ears, the flash grenades weren't going to have an effect.

Lula put her hands to her head. "Where's my Farrah Fawcett wig? Someone took my wig. I'm pressing charges. Don't anybody leave the scene."

There were a bunch of signs scattered around, but not many protesters. Slick was gone and so were my handcuffs. The police and some Parks were cleaning up the litter. No blond wig in sight.

"It was splattered with tomato, anyway," I said.

"Yeah, you got some on you too. And egg. And your shirt got a big rip in it. I'm sayin' that all in all this here was a depressing day. I need a donut."

A donut sounded like a good idea. A dozen donuts sounded even better. It was almost nine o'clock, and the sun had set. I wasn't sure if I was up for the late dinner with Morelli. I was hungry, but I wasn't feeling like a sex goddess. I was feeling like I'd gotten punched in the face, and my eye was swelling.

"Do I have a black eye?" I asked Lula.

"I can't tell," Lula said. "It's too dark here."

We walked for two blocks and stopped.

"Where's your car?" Lula asked. "I could swear we parked it here."

We looked around. No car.

"I think someone stole your car," Lula said.

"I think you're right."

"This is doodie," Lula said. "Just when I need a donut someone goes and steals your car. Some people have no consideration."

I reviewed my choices. I could call Morelli. I could call my dad. I could call Uber. Or I could call Ranger.

"Hold on," Lula said. "What's that laying in the gutter? Looks to me like your license plates."

I went to the curb and retrieved the plates.

"This is looking up," Lula said. "At least you got your plates. All we need now is a car. How about the one across the street. It looks like a Lexus."

"We aren't going to steal a car."

"I don't see why not. Someone took ours, so we should be able to help ourself to a new one. Tit for tat."

My cellphone buzzed, and the screen told me it was Ranger. Ricardo Carlos Manoso, aka Ranger, is former Special Forces. He's smart. He's sexy. He's Cuban American. He grew up street tough. He has his own moral code. And he has secrets. He wears only black unless he's undercover. He sits with his back to the wall when he's in a public place.

When we first met, Ranger was working as a bounty hunter. Since then he's become a successful businessman, owning and operating Rangeman, a high-tech security firm housed in a stealth building in downtown Trenton. We've been intimate in the past, but much like with Diesel, there's no possibility of marriage or even a long-term, stable relationship. Ranger has complicated life goals. He also has an overly protective attitude, and he puts trackers on my cars so he can keep tabs on me. I've given up trying to remove them.

"My control room tells me your car just went for a swim in the Delaware River," Ranger said.

"It was just stolen. You should probably send the police to see if there's anyone in it."

"Do you need a ride?"

I blew out a sigh. "Yes. And I have Lula with me. Do you know where I am?"

"State and Lincoln."

I narrowed my eyes. "Do you have my messenger bag bugged again?"

"No. I can ping your cellphone."

"Is Mr. Tall, Dark, and Hot coming to get us?" Lula asked after I put my phone back into my pocket.

"Yep."

"Even better than stealing a car. That man is fine."

. . .

Lula and I were sitting on the curb when Ranger eased to a stop in front of us in his black Porsche Cayenne turbo. I slid into the seat next to him, he studied me in the dark car, and he almost smiled.

"Babe," Ranger said.

Babe covered a lot of ground with Ranger. I was guessing tonight it meant I was a mess.

"We got involved in a demonstration," I said.

When Ranger was working as a bounty hunter he'd had a diamond stud in his ear and his hair pulled back into a ponytail. He's a businessman now, and he's always perfectly groomed and tailored. No more diamond stud and no more ponytail. Today he was wearing the Rangeman uniform of black fatigues.

"And some loser took my Farrah wig right off my head," Lula said. "That's why I don't look completely put together."

Ranger flicked his eyes to the rearview mirror and returned his attention to the road. Twenty minutes later he dropped Lula at her house. He waited until she walked inside and closed her door before turning to me.

"You have the beginnings of a black eye, your shirt is ripped, and you look hungry," Ranger said. "Where do we go from here? Would you like to come home with me, or do you have other plans?"

I leaned back in the seat and closed my eyes. "I suppose I have other plans. I should go back to my apartment."

Ranger drove in silence. Never a man of many words. More of an action kind of guy. He pulled into the parking lot to my apartment building and looked up at my windows on the second floor.

"Did you leave your lights on?" he asked.

I gave up a sigh. "Diesel showed up today."

"And?"

"And I'm guessing he's still here."

"Would you like me to remove him?"

"No. I'll take care of it."

"Babe," Ranger said. "You don't want to get involved with Diesel."

"No problem. Not a chance."

He looked down at the license plates that were resting on my lap. "They left the plates behind?"

"Yep."

"Thoughtful." He leaned in and kissed me, being careful of the eye. "I'll have one of my men drop a car off for you."

"Thanks. I'll try not to lose it."

"If you can manage to keep it intact for a week, it's yours. If it gets stolen, blown up, crushed by a garbage truck, set on fire, filled with cement, or dies an untimely death by any other means, I'll expect you to spend the night with me."

I got out of his Cayenne and watched him drive away. It would be tempting to blow the car up myself.

. . .

Diesel was slouched on my couch, watching television, when I let myself into my apartment. He stood and stretched, his shirt rode up exposing his perfect abs, and I sucked in some air. I had too many men in my life. And none of them were doing me any good.

I put the plates on the kitchen counter, tapped on Rex's cage, and said hello. Diesel strolled in and did a head-to-toe body scan.

"What's the other guy look like?" he asked.

"There were multiple other guys. I'm not sure what they looked like. It was dark and chaotic."

"Was it fun?"

"Not especially."

He opened some kitchen drawers until he found a tea towel. He loaded it with ice, smashed the ice with a fry pan, and gently put the towel to my swollen black eye.

"Are you hungry?"

"Yes!"

He poured me a glass of red wine, took two mac and cheese boxes out of the freezer, and popped them into the microwave. He sliced the hot dogs, put them in the defrosted mac and cheese, and nuked it all for another minute. He dumped one box onto a plate for me and the other onto a plate for him.

"Instant happiness," he said, draping an arm around me,

shepherding me into the living room. "The Yankees are losing. It's all good."

"You're not a Yankees fan?"

"Red Sox."

I forked into my frank and cheese. "Who would have thought you could cook?"

"Just the tip of the iceberg."

"No doubt."

I ate my dinner, drank my wine, and put the ice pack back on my eye.

"Do you want to talk about it?" Diesel asked.

"No. It's not that interesting."

"You've got something on your forehead and in your hair. It's either raw egg or else someone got happy on you."

"It's egg. I guess I should take a shower and wash it out."

"Let me know if you need help," Diesel said. "I'm good in the shower."

I shuffled off to the bathroom and cringed when I saw myself in the mirror. My eye was swollen and ringed with deep purple. My T-shirt was ripped at the neck. My hair was spiked with egg goo.

This is no way to live, I told myself. There must be a better way to pay the rent. When my face stopped throbbing I was going to think about it.

I called Morelli and told him I was going to pass on the dinner thing. For starters, I didn't have a car.

"Rekko said he saw you at the Korean grocery protest. He said you started a riot."

"I wasn't the one who started the riot. I tried to make an

apprehension and it went south, and then one thing led to another. How's the head count going?"

"It's going freaky. Bad enough we've got these heads in cold storage, it turns out they haven't got brains."

"Say what?"

"I'm not going to repeat it. I shouldn't have told you because it hasn't been released, but I'm creeped out, and I've had two whiskeys straight up. No fucking brains."

"Do you think it's the zombies?"

"No. I think it's some sick psychotic asshole. Or maybe a bunch of assholes. Or hell, I guess it could be zombies."

"I still haven't found Ethel."

"I'd like to help, but I haven't got time. I'm pulling double shifts, running down decapitation leads."

"Grandma will be happy when you find the head thief. Leonard Friedman had to have a closed casket. And you know how Grandma hates a closed casket."

"I knew Leonard. A closed casket would have been a good idea even if his head was attached. He wasn't an attractive man."

I said good night to Morelli and stepped into the shower. I have an ugly 1970s-era bathroom. I tell myself the avocado wallpaper and baby-diarrhea yellow fixtures are retro, but truth is they were a bad idea in the '70s and they're a worse idea now. I scrubbed the egg away and stood under the hot water until it started to go cold. I toweled off, blasted my hair with the dryer, got into my pajamas, and went out to see if Diesel was still in my living room.

"Yeah, I'm still here," he said. "Come cuddle."

"Gonna pass on the cuddling and go straight to bed."

"Is that an invitation?"

"No. It's a declaration. I'm beat." I put my finger to my eye and tested it for puffiness. "How does my eye look?"

"It looks like you smashed it into someone's fist."

SIX

I WOKE UP a little after midnight and realized I was in bed alone, and there were no television sounds drifting under my door. I got out of bed and walked through my apartment. No Diesel. Lights were off. The front door was locked. Rex was running on his wheel. On my way back to bed I caught sight of Diesel's beat-up knapsack resting against the side of the couch. He was gone but not forever.

The next time I awoke it was morning. The sun was shining, and Diesel was sleeping peacefully beside me. His arm was draped across my chest. The clothes he'd been wearing were on the floor. All of them.

Best to sneak out of bed before he wakes up and gets amorous, I thought. I maneuvered out from under the arm and tiptoed into the bathroom. When I emerged a half hour later I was dressed and ready to start my day, and Diesel was still asleep. I made coffee, and ate a peanut butter and banana sandwich. I returned to the bathroom to brush my teeth and take another look at my eye. The swelling was down but the bruise was worse. Diesel was still sleeping.

"Hey!" I shouted, standing over him.

He rolled over onto his back and opened his eyes. "What?"

"Just wanted to make sure you weren't dead."

"Late night," he said. "I smell coffee."

"Where were you?"

"Working."

"Night watchman?"

"More or less." He threw the covers off, stood, and stretched.

"God's sake!" I said. "Don't you have *any modesty*?"

"None. You just noticed?"

I noticed lots of things. Actually, *everything*. The man was stupefyingly gorgeous.

"I'm going to work," I said. "Will you still be here when I return?"

"Probably. You might want to pick up more mac and cheese."

He padded off to the bathroom, and I left the apartment. I walked out into the parking lot and realized I didn't have a car. A moment later a black Mercedes SUV pulled up in front of me and stopped. A Rangeman guy got out and handed me a key fob.

"From Ranger," he said. "Registration is in the glove compartment, and it's equipped with the usual."

That meant it had a GPS tracker stuck somewhere, and a loaded gun in a lockbox under the driver's seat.

A black Ford Explorer drove up, the Rangeman guy got in, and the SUV left the parking lot.

. . .

Lula was already at the office when I arrived.

"Whoa," she said. "You got a hideous eye."

"The swelling is down and my nose doesn't feel broken."

"Yeah, your nose looks okay. Good thing too because you have an excellent nose. People pay big money to get a nose like that."

"Anything new?" I asked Connie.

Connie looked up from her computer. "No new FTAs, but my cousin Miriam told me that the funeral home on Liberty Street lost two heads last night. Miriam works there as a cosmetologist. She came to work this morning to get Mrs. Werner and Mr. Shantz ready for their viewings and when they pulled them out of the drawer they didn't have their heads."

"I don't like this," Lula said. "This is creeping me out. Who goes around taking dead people's heads? It's just not right. Hold on, do you think it's terrorists?"

"Unlikely," Connie said. "These people were already dead."

"Maybe they were practicing," Lula said. "Like the way medical students do on cadavers."

I took a donut from the box on Connie's desk. "I have my own problems. I need to find Diggery's snake."

"I'd rather look for the missing heads," Lula said. "I don't like snakes. And I especially don't like *big* snakes."

"You can stay in the car," I said.

"Whose car we talking about?"

"My car. The one that's parked at the curb."

Lula looked out the large plate glass window. "There's a Mercedes out there."

"It's from Ranger."

"That's one of them little GLE SUVs. That car's the bomb. And it's all new and shiny. It's almost as good as my Firebird."

"Remember Johnny Chucci?" Connie asked me.

I nodded yes. "He robbed the jewelry store on State. The one by the porn store."

"He's the dude who wears underpants on his head," Lula said. "He didn't just rob the jewelry store. He robbed the porn store too. Except we're not supposed to call it a 'porn store' nowadays. The politically correct name is 'adult entertainment emporium.' They even got that on a new sign. Anyways, they caught him with his pockets full of cock rings. Not that I know why any man would want more than one cock ring, but what the heck."

"He skipped out and stuck us with his bail bond," Connie said. "Left the area, and we had no luck tracing him. It's been almost a year, but there are rumors that he's back in town. We might be able to collect some of the bond if you could bring him in. It was armed robbery, so he's worth money."

"I'm sure I have his file at home," I said.

Connie tapped "C-h-u-c-c-i" into her computer. "I'll print out a new one for you."

"He should be easy to spot if he's still wearing his Fruit of the Looms like a ski mask," Lula said.

"He only did that when he was robbing something," I said. "It was his signature statement."

"It was his nutcase statement," Lula said. "He couldn't see with them on. He got caught on account of he fell off the curb when he ran out of the adult emporium."

I took the file from Connie, and Lula and I headed out in the Mercedes. First stop would be Diggeryville. Get the snake responsibility over first.

"That snake could be anywhere by now," Lula said. "It could be in Delaware."

"Usually a pet will stay close to home," I said.

"It might be different if there's zombies around. Ethel might be worried about her brain. Okay, so it's about as big as a walnut, but it might still make a good zombie snack."

I crept down the rutted dirt road, looking side to side. I parked in Diggery's yard, got out, and looked around. No boa in a tree. No boa sunning herself in front of the double-wide stoop. I cautiously walked to the makeshift steps and peeked through the open door. No boa in sight.

BEEP! BEEP! BEEP!

Lula was blowing the horn and waving at me. Frantic. I could see her mouth working, and knew she was yelling something at me, but I couldn't hear over the horn beeping.

I ran back to the SUV and got in.

"Get me out of here," Lula said. "Go *now*! I saw them. They were coming to get me."

"Who?"

"The zombies. I saw them. Two of them. All raggedy and

dead looking. Their eyes were red and glowing and sunken in, and the one had a big hole in his forehead. That's probably where some other zombie sucked out his brain."

I looked around. "I don't see any zombies."

"They went back into the woods when I started blowing the horn. They were horrible! I could even smell them. They smelled like dirt and mold and rotting carnations."

"Carnations?"

"Yeah. I'm thinking they were the funeral home head robbers, and they picked up the carnation stench while they were there."

I put the SUV in gear and drove back to the main road, being careful not to run over any zombies.

"Maybe you nodded off and *dreamed* there were zombies," I said to Lula.

"I wasn't nodded off. I know what I saw, and I saw zombies. And I didn't like the way they were looking at me. Like I was lunch or something. Like they wanted to suck out my brain. You know how when men get scared, their gonads shrink up inside their body? That's how my brain was feeling. If my brain was a gonad it'd be all sneaked up behind my kidneys."

"Good thing it's not a gonad then."

"You bet your ass," Lula said.

I turned onto State Street. "Johnny Chucci and Zero Slick are in the wind. Pick your poison," I said. "Who's first on our list?"

"I got a real interest in Zero Slick. He looks like an unpleasant chubby little nerd, but he picked himself an excellent name. He's like an enigma, right?"

I thought he was more loser than enigma but hell, who am I to judge.

"We haven't got much to go on with him," I said. "He doesn't have an address, but he seems to have a neighborhood. I guess we could ride around the building he blew up and see if we get lucky."

I was a block away when Connie called me.

"I'm listening to the police band, and a call just came in about a boa spotted on the three hundred block of Pilkman Street," Connie said. "Pilkman backs up to the patch of woods by Diggery's double-wide. If you hurry you could get there ahead of animal control."

I made an instant U-turn. "I'm on it."

"I'm not on it," Lula said. "I'm not in favor of this. Suppose it's Ethel? Then what? You gonna escort her into your Mercedes and put a seatbelt on her? You gonna talk her into turning around and following you through zombie country, back to Diggery's place?"

"I'll think of something."

"We don't even have any snake-catching equipment with us. We don't have one of those loop things you see on the nature channel. We don't have no rats or chickens or roadkill to feed it. We don't got a snake cage. I don't even know what a snake cage looks like. The snakes at the zoo are behind glass."

"I'll stun-gun her."

"Say what?"

"I'll zap Ethel with my stun gun, load her into the back of the SUV, and take her home to Diggery's double-wide."

"Are you nuts?"

"It could work."

"What about salmonella?" Lula said. "You could get salmonella from touching a snake."

"I have hand sanitizer in my messenger bag."

SEVEN

LULA WAS ON the alert when I turned onto Pilkman.

"There's three women standing on the sidewalk on the next block," she said. "I'm guessing they're snake watching."

I parked near the women, and Lula and I got out. A huge snake was curled up on a patch of grass that served as front yard to a modest bungalow.

"What do you think?" I asked Lula. "Is that Ethel?"

"Hard to tell," Lula said. "Last I saw her she was draped in a tree."

"It's a boa," one of the women said. "We looked it up."

"Have you ever seen this snake around here before?" I asked her. "Does anyone in this neighborhood own a snake?"

Everyone shook their head. No one had seen the snake before today.

"Hey! Ethel!" Lula shouted at the snake.

We all took a step closer and looked to see if there was any response.

"It opened an eye," Lula said. "That's Ethel all right."

"Is Ethel your snake?" the woman asked.

"She belongs to someone we know," Lula said. "And Stephanie here is responsible for bringing her home."

"It's an awfully big snake," one of the other women said.

"Yeah, but Stephanie's got a plan," Lula said. "She's gonna load Ethel into the back of her car. I know that Mercedes looks like a luxury vehicle, but it's got some muscle, and if we keep Ethel all curled up, we're pretty sure she'll fit."

My heart was beating with a sickening *thud*. I was terrified of Ethel. And I was repulsed at the thought of touching her.

Okay, I told myself. Attitude adjustment needed. She's a pet. She's had a big adventure, and she'll be happy to go home. And she doesn't look hungry, so that's a good thing. Most likely she's just eaten a beagle, and she's feeling sleepy. No reason to be afraid. And probably she feels good to the touch. You wouldn't have a problem if she was a pair of cowboy boots, right?

I inched closer, telling myself to stay calm. I circled around to Ethel's tail and took a deep breath. I reached down to touch her, and she tensed, raised her head, and looked at me. I stumbled back and paused for a moment, relieved that I hadn't soiled myself.

"Maybe you shouldn't get so close," one of the women said. "Maybe you should wait for animal control."

"No worries," Lula said. "Stephanie knows what she's doing. Besides, Ethel's just saying hello."

Ethel was uncurling and moving toward me, eyes wide open, forked tongue out. I didn't see any lumps in her body that would indicate the presence of an undigested beagle, and I was thinking I might be wrong about her not being hungry. I had pepper spray in one hand and my stun gun in my other hand, and I had no idea if either would have any effect on a boa.

"You grab her, and I'll go open the back door," Lula said.

"Here's the deal," I said to Ethel. "I promised Diggery I'd sort of take care of you while he was locked up. So I have to get you back to the double-wide. And that means I have to get you into my car. And that means I have to immobilize you a little. I swear to God, it'll be okay, and after I get you home I'll bring you a pizza. It's the best I can do because the rats got all eaten."

Ethel lunged at me, and I gave her a bunch of jolts with the stun gun. She shuddered and twitched, her head hit the ground, and she didn't move.

"What did you do?" one of the women said. "Is she dead?"

"She's stunned," I said.

I wrapped my hands around Ethel's tail and tried to pull her toward the car, but it was like moving a fifty-pound sandbag.

"I need help," I said. "I can't move her all by myself."

No one came forward.

"She's currently on someone's front lawn," I said.

A woman with short brown hair raised her hand.

"If you want her off your lawn you're going to have to help me move her."

"What the heck?" the woman said. "I have three out-of-control kids and a three-hundred-pound husband who snores like a yeti. I guess I can move a snake."

Everyone but Lula grabbed a piece of Ethel. We wrestled her into the back of the Mercedes and closed the door on her.

"Appreciate the help, ladies," I said. "I'm sure Ethel will be happy to get home."

I jumped behind the wheel, and Lula got in beside me.

"That went off easy-peasy," Lula said. "Bing bang bam. Are we a team, or what? Now all we got to do is get Ethel into the double-wide. I bet you got a plan for that too."

"I have hot dogs. And I promised her pizza."

"That would do it for me."

I turned onto State, drove for ten minutes, and turned onto Diggery's road.

"This could be a new profession for us," Lula said. "We could be snake wranglers. I bet there's good money in it."

"I think I hear some rustling in the back. Check on Ethel for me. See if she's okay."

"It's just this bumpy, crap-ass road," Lula said. "Ethel's sleeping like a baby."

"Still, just turn around and make sure."

"No problem. *YOW! She's awake. Lordy, she's coming to get me. She's going to eat me alive!*"

"Don't panic. Take my stun gun and give her another shot of electric."

"Let me out. Stop the car."

In my peripheral vision, I saw a snake head slither over Lula's shoulder.

"*YOW!*" Lula shrieked, flailing her arms. "*Let me out of here!*"

Lula jumped out of the moving car. The snake slid onto the floor and over my foot. I went into a freak-out, the SUV veered off the road, and I crashed into an outhouse that belonged to one of the yurt people. I fought my way free of the inflated airbag, opened my door, tumbled out, and the snake zigzagged over me and disappeared into the woods.

I lay there for a full minute, struggling to breathe, before Lula gave me a hand-up and pulled me to my feet.

"This stinks," Lula said.

"I know. The snake got away."

"No. I mean it *really stinks*. You trashed an outhouse."

The entire front end of the Mercedes was bashed in, and the SUV was resting on the outhouse remains. Both the outhouse and the SUV were leaking. I rescued my messenger bag from the car and called Ranger.

"It wasn't my fault," I said. "There was a snake in the car."

"Babe, you've had the car for less than two hours."

Lula was backing away, holding her nose and fanning the air.

"If you're sending someone to take care of this you'll want to send him in a hazmat suit," I said to Ranger. "I sort of ran over an outhouse."

There was silence on the other end.

"Hello?" I said. "Are you still there? Do I hear you laughing?"

"You never disappoint," Ranger said.

An hour later, Lula was loaded into a Rangeman SUV and shuttled off to the office. The Mercedes was winched onto a flatbed tow truck. And Ranger and I were in his Cayenne, watching Ethel follow the newly laid out trail of hot dogs that led into Diggery's double-wide. When all of Ethel was inside, I ran to the door, told her I'd be back with her pizza, and locked her in.

"Finally," I said to Ranger. "Success."

"I was thinking the same thing. You owe me a night."

"Maybe not. The car might not be totaled."

"Babe, you rolled it over an outhouse."

"I don't suppose you'd want to give me another chance?"

Ranger smiled. "Double or nothing."

"Deal."

EIGHT

RANGER DROVE ME home and parked in the lot behind my building.

"Diesel is still there," Ranger said, looking up at my second-floor apartment windows.

"How do you know?"

"I just know."

"What's this strange connection between the two of you?"

"There's no connection," Ranger said. "We've crossed paths."

"You don't like him."

Ranger studied me for a beat. "I understand him. I know who he is."

"He's like you," I said.

"In some ways."

"That's pretty scary right there."

Ranger leaned in and kissed me. "You have no idea."

I left Ranger and trudged off to my apartment. Diesel was sprawled on the couch when I walked in.

"I'm taking a shower," I said on my way to the bathroom.

"Good move," Diesel said. "You smell like an outhouse."

I stopped and looked at him.

"Lucky guess," Diesel said.

"How's the disturbance in the force? Is it getting better?"

"It's getting worse."

I gave up a sigh and locked myself in the bathroom. I stuffed my clothes into a plastic trash bag, shampooed my hair three times, and stepped out of the shower feeling like a new woman. I got dressed, pulled my hair into a ponytail, and set out to start my day . . . again.

Diesel was gone when I walked out of the bedroom. No doubt he was skulking around somewhere, checking on the force. I made myself another peanut butter sandwich and looked out my living room window, down at the parking lot. There were two black SUVs idling near the building's back door. One was clearly a Rangeman vehicle. The other was smaller. Hard to tell the make from my vantage point. A Rangeman guy stood by the smaller car. I grabbed my messenger bag and went downstairs.

"From Ranger," the Rangeman guy said, handing me the key.

It was a Lexus NX 330 F Sport. Shiny new. Didn't smell like an outhouse. I got behind the wheel, and Ranger's men drove off. My plan was to retrieve Lula from the bonds office, take a pizza to Ethel, and hunt down Johnny Chucci.

Lula was pacing when I got to the office.

"I've got the creeps," she said. "I feel like I'm being followed. Like someone's spying on me."

"Who?" I asked.

"I don't know," Lula said. "It's just one of them feelings."

Connie looked at me and rolled her eyes. This was just short of making one of those circular motions with your finger alongside your head to signify crazy.

"Maybe you're hungry," I said to Lula. "I promised Ethel I'd bring her a pizza. We could get one for you too."

"I'd never refuse a pizza," Lula said. "Especially if it was a Pino's pizza."

Twenty minutes later I was on my way to Diggery's. Lula had a pizza with the works in a box on her lap, and there was a sausage and extra cheese on the back seat for Ethel. I had her figured for a meat lover.

"I'm feeling better already," Lula said, selecting a second piece. "I don't know what came over me. It was like my skin was crawling. You ever get that? I mean, I'm not necessarily a nervous person. I don't have any of them panic attacks, so this was weird. I just knew something was wrong."

"But it's not wrong now?"

"Not so much. I'm settling in with the pizza. You could always count on melted cheese to have a calming effect."

I turned onto Diggery's road and cringed when I passed the demolished outhouse. Not one of my finer moments.

"It was a lucky break that Ethel decided to go home," Lula said. "I have to tell you until that happened I wasn't sure it was Ethel."

And it was still possible that it wasn't Ethel. The only thing I knew for certain was that the snake liked hot dogs.

I parked close to Diggery's front door and did a fast scan for snakes and zombies. I didn't see either, so I gave the pizza to the snake in residence and took off.

"I suppose we'll go looking for Zero Slick now," Lula said. "How do you think he came up with a name like that?"

"Maybe that's the way he thinks of himself. Zero slickness."

"That might indicate low self-esteem. He could be a man trying to find himself. He could be a victim of bullying at a young age. Or maybe he doesn't want to be one of those phony slick guys. Maybe he's saying he's real. If you look at it that way he could be attractively manly."

"He didn't look attractively manly when he hit me with his sign. He looked like a brainless jerk."

"You got a point. And he was insulting about my abundant body. He might be losing some of his appeal for me."

My plan was to walk the streets surrounding the building Slick destroyed. This was an area of mostly office buildings with occasional ground-floor shops. There was a church nearby that gave out sandwiches to the homeless every day at noon. A small group of men and women never left the area around the church. They moved about like pack animals, sleeping in doorways. Some were crazy because they were off their meds, and others were crazy because they were overmedicated. I thought I'd show Slick's photo to the crazies, the shopkeepers, and the loiterers and see if anyone had seen him.

I approached the burned-out building and saw the flashing lights of police cruisers a block away.

"Looks like something's going on at the homeless church," Lula said. "Maybe it's a wedding."

"Looks more like a crime scene. There's a CSI truck and the ME's truck stuck in with the cruisers. And it looks like Morelli's SUV is parked off to the side."

I pulled to the curb, Lula and I got out, and walked to the church. A couple uniforms were standing hands-on-hips by the cars, but most of the activity was in the back alley. I could see yellow crime scene tape cordoning off an area. Morelli was there, watching the CSI techs work around what I suspected was a body. I ducked under the tape and walked over to Morelli, standing with my back to the body, not anxious to see the victim.

"What's going on?" I asked him.

"One of the church volunteers came out with trash from lunch and found a homeless man stretched out next to the dumpster. He was one of the regulars who lived on the street."

"Dead?"

"Yep."

I was afraid to ask. "Headless?"

"No," Morelli said. "He still had his head, but someone drilled a hole in the skull, and it appears that the brain might have gotten sucked out. Won't know for sure until the autopsy."

A wave of nausea slid through my stomach, and I went light-headed for a moment.

"Are you okay?" Morelli asked.

"No. I'm not okay. That's horrible."

"At least they left the head this time. Makes my job easier."

"Do you have any leads on this?"

"Not a one," Morelli said.

"Lula thinks it's zombies."

"Okay, so now I have one lead. Does she have an address for the zombies?"

"They originally came from the cemetery on Morley Street, but I'm not sure where they're hanging out now."

"Well, that's a start. I'll check out Morley Street."

I grimaced and looked at him. "You're kidding, right?"

"Yes. I'm kidding. There's some psycho nutjob out there collecting cadaver brains."

"So I'm safe as long as I'm not dead?"

"Looks that way."

"I guess that's comforting."

"Not to me. The department is working overtime to keep this out of the press, and the mayor is on everyone's ass to find the idiot who's doing it." His expression softened, and he gently touched my cheek with his fingertip. "Your eye looks awful."

"Zero Slick hit me with his protest sign."

"He's an asshole. Do you want me to bring him in and charge him?"

"No. I'll take care of it. You have your own problems."

"Cupcake, *you're* my problem."

"I don't want to be your problem. I want to be your sex goddess."

This got a smile out of Morelli. "You're all that and more."

I gave him a small kiss and a smile. "Gotta go. Probably I won't see you tonight?"

"Not likely."

"Okeydokey then," I said, relieved that I didn't have to address the Diesel issue.

Lula was waiting on the other side of the crime scene tape. "What's up?" she asked.

"Homeless man is dead."

"And? There's a lot going on for a dead homeless man."

"He might be missing his brain."

"Say what? Holy crapola. It's the zombies, isn't it? They came and sucked out his brain. I knew it. I could feel something was happening. I told you, right? I was creeped out. I knew they were roaming around. I bet they wanted my brain, but it wasn't available, so they went somewhere else."

"Zombies aren't on the short list for the police. They're thinking more lunatic."

"They don't know nothing. This here's the work of zombies. Anybody could see that."

I didn't know which was worse . . . a criminally insane cannibal or a hungry zombie. Hard to believe that either existed.

"This neighborhood seems to be congested," I said to Lula. "I'm thinking we change direction and look for Johnny Chucci."

"Whatever. I'm a flexible person. There's probably zombies lurking here anyway. Now that I'm thinking about it I can feel them looking at me. You probably want to take some evasive action when you drive out of here."

"You think zombies can drive?"

"I'm thinking it's possible."

"Can they only drive forward?"

"I don't know," Lula said. "That would be one of them zombie mysteries."

I hung a U-turn and drove to the Burg. Johnny Chucci's mother lives in the Burg. His sister lives in the Burg. His two brothers live in the Burg. His ex-wife lives in the Burg. If Johnny was back, sooner or later, he'd be in the Burg, if not to live at least to visit.

"I guess you know Johnny Chucci," Lula said.

"Not personally. He's a couple years older than me. Grandma Mazur knows his mom. She sees her at bingo and the funeral home sometimes. I know about the family from Grandma Mazur."

"Your granny knows everything," Lula said. "When I grow up I want to be just like her."

I passed the Chucci file over to Lula. "The family addresses should be listed. I know where the mother lives. I can't remember the others."

"You gonna just drive around?"

"Yes. And then I'll decide if I want to talk to anyone."

"I think you should talk to your granny. It would have the added benefit of a piece of coffee cake or some of them Italian cookies. There's always excellent bakery products at your momma's house."

I'd had the same thoughts. Grandma was tapped into the Burg gossip network. There was a good possibility she knew something about Johnny Chucci. And, more important, I could use a cookie.

Johnny's parents lived in a two-story frame house that was similar in size to my parents' house. It had a postage stamp front yard, a small front porch, and a single-car detached garage at the rear of their property. There was a blue F-150 pickup parked in the driveway.

"This is a nice house," Lula said. "It's all kept up with fresh paint, and they even got a pot of flowers on the porch."

"Do we have an address for his sister?"

"She's two houses down on the same side of the street. It's the house that's painted blue and has the big American flag hanging on the front porch and the kids' toys on the sidewalk. If I had a house of my own I'd fly a flag. It'd be a big one too, on account of I'm not a halfway person. And I'm all for being patriotic."

"What about the ex-wife?"

"The ex-wife, Judy, is on South Street."

South Street was on the other side of the Burg and one block away from my parents' house. Convenient for the cookie drop-in. I followed the familiar maze of streets to South Street and idled in front of Judy Chucci's house.

"Holy cow," Lula said. "She's got gnomes all over her front lawn. It's a gnome-con. There must be forty gnomes here. They're all painted the same, too. Red hats and blue pants. I guess that's classic gnome colors." Lula shifted in her seat. "You ever notice that Trenton has some strange stuff going on? Clusters of gnomes and zombies. Trenton could be like *Ghostbusters,* where all the paranormal apparitions get together in one spot, and one day *BOOM*. All hell breaks loose, and we get overrun by funky-ass gnomes."

I glanced over at Lula. "You realize those gnomes aren't real, right? They're made of plaster, and she probably got them at the flea market."

"Okay, but who knows what happens at night? They could come alive like the zombies."

I turned the corner and drove to my parents' house. "You need cake."

"Hell, yeah."

NINE

GRANDMA WAS AT the door when Lula and I set foot on the porch. "I was hoping someone would come to visit," Grandma said. "The television is on the blink, and there are no viewings at the funeral home today. I got nothing to do."

"How come there are no viewings?" Lula asked. "Seems like there are always viewings."

"The word is that they're working overtime at Stiva's trying to get Emily Molinowski's head back on her. She's supposed to have a viewing tonight, and they're advertising an open casket. The funeral home is going to be packed. I'm going a half hour early or I won't get a good seat."

We all made our way back to the kitchen, where my mother was putting a meatloaf together.

"Sit down and I'll get the cookies," Grandma said to Lula and me.

Lula took a seat at the small kitchen table. "We just passed by a house with a whole bunch of gnomes in the front yard. What's with that?"

"You must be talking about Judy Chucci," Grandma said, setting out a bakery box of Italian cookies. "She's a little nutty with the gnomes. Gets them at the craft store and paints them herself. The inside of her house is filled with them. She said she needed a hobby after the divorce from Johnny. And then she had that accident at work and went on disability. I guess now she sits home all day painting gnomes."

"What kind of a disability does she have?"

"She worked at the button factory. One of the machines went haywire and spewed oil on her, and she slipped and fell down and broke her back."

"That's horrible," Lula said.

"I think it was only broke a little," Grandma said. "She was laid up for a couple weeks, but she seems to get around okay now. I imagine she'll be on disability until the lawsuit is settled with the button factory."

I took a cookie from the box. "Does she still see Johnny?"

"Not that I know about," Grandma said. "It was a nasty divorce. Not as nasty as yours. Your divorce was epic. Still, hers was pretty good."

"The Chuccis had a custody dispute over the dog," my mother said. "It dragged on for a year."

"How was it resolved?" Lula asked.

"The dog died. Choked on a chicken bone," my mother said.

"That's so sad," Lula said. "They should have been more careful about giving that dog bones."

"As I remember, it got into the garbage when Judy was off at work," Grandma said. "It was a hound dog."

"That explains it," Lula said. "My uncle had a hound, and it ate everything."

"Connie heard that Johnny was back in town," I said. "He skipped out on Vinnie right before his court date. It was a high bond, and we might recover some of it if I could find Johnny."

"I'm on it," Grandma said. "I'll sleuth around tonight at the Molinowski viewing. If Johnny shows up I'll take him down for you."

"You will do no such thing," my mother said to Grandma. "And I'm checking your purse when you go out to make sure you don't have a gun in it."

Grandma winked at me when my mom wasn't looking. She would have the gun wedged into her underwear until she got to the funeral home, and then would transfer it to her purse. Grandma *always* packed. She packed when she went to the bakery. She lived for the chance to say, *"Make my day, punk."*

"Who are you tracking down these days besides Johnny?" Grandma asked.

"Zero Slick is out there," Lula said. "We started looking for him, but his neighborhood is all blocked off on account of some homeless guy got his brain sucked out."

"Damn zombies," Grandma said. "They're running amuck all over the place. Grace Merkle said she saw one tramping through her flower garden the other night. She lives two blocks from the cemetery on Morley Street. She said the zombies are a real nuisance."

My mother looked over at the cabinet where she kept her whiskey. She checked her watch. Too early for a drink. There were rules to be observed. Good Christian women didn't drink before four o'clock unless they were at a wake. My mother gave up a small sigh and took a cookie.

"You could probably bend the rules, since there are zombies in Grace Merkle's flower garden," I said to my mother.

"I've got fifteen minutes to go," my mother said, taking a second cookie. "I can stick it out."

"Boy, you're a strong woman," Lula said. "You got real willpower."

"The rules change when you get to be a senior citizen," Grandma said. "If I want a snort of whiskey in the morning I go for it. I probably only got about thirty good years left."

By my calculations, thirty good years had Grandma well over a hundred. No doubt in my mind that she would still be going strong.

"My honey just took a part-time job as a greeter," Grandma said. "He's working in one of those bars in Key West."

"You got a honey?" Lula asked.

"I met him on one of them Internet sites," Grandma said. "He's a real looker."

"You gotta be careful of those Internet hookups," Lula said.

Grandma pulled the picture up on her cellphone and showed Lula.

"That's George Hamilton," Lula said.

"Yeah, there's a good resemblance," Grandma said. "I'm guessing he's a little younger than me, but I think I can keep up."

"What's a greeter do for a bar?" Lula asked.

"It sounds to me like he holds up a sign outside saying that they got cheap drinks and live dancers inside," Grandma said. "He works days, so I'm thinking it'll help him keep that deep tan he's got."

"No doubt," Lula said.

My mother crammed two more cookies into her mouth.

"Okay then," I said. "This has been nice, but Lula and I have to move on. It's about quitting time."

"Don't worry," Grandma said. "You can count on me to find out about Johnny."

"Thanks," I said. "I'd appreciate any information you can get, but please don't shoot anyone."

"Not unless I have to," Grandma said.

"Can't ask for more than that," Lula said.

I gave my mother a hug, told her to hang in there, and maneuvered Lula out of the house and into my car.

"Your granny is a hoot," Lula said, buckling herself in. "And imagine snagging a guy who looks like George Hamilton. How cool is that? Are you gonna look up Johnny's two brothers?"

"Not today."

I drove back to the building Slick destroyed. The crime scene tape was still up, and the CSI people were working. Morelli's car was still there. I cruised the perimeter and didn't see Slick, so I took Lula back to the office.

"See you tomorrow," Lula said. "Have a good night."

That was worth an eye roll. I had Diesel squatting in my apartment, and my grandmother was going to Emily

Molinowski's viewing with a loaded gun. Not that it was entirely my fault. She would have gone with a loaded gun as a matter of habit. Problem is, now she was on the hunt for Johnny Chucci. It had seemed like a good idea to ask if she'd heard anything. In retrospect, maybe not smart.

This wasn't going to be a good night.

• • •

My apartment was empty when I walked in. No Diesel. No Morelli. No Ranger. Just Rex asleep in his soup can. I tapped on the side of his cage and said hello.

No answer from Rex.

I opened my laptop and checked my email. I wasted a half hour on Facebook. I logged into a search engine and researched Johnny Chucci and his relatives. Ditto Zero Slick. I didn't get anything new on Chucci. Slick had applied for a car loan and been declined. Possibly he was declined because he listed his address as "Under the bridge."

I shuffled off to the kitchen and stared into the refrigerator. I couldn't get excited about another peanut butter sandwich. Yogurt, no. Cereal, no. Ham sandwich, no. I grabbed a bottle of beer, took a step back, bumped into Diesel, and yelped in surprise.

"Jeez Louise," I said. "I hate when you sneak up on me like that. I didn't hear you come in."

"You were in the zone."

"I was contemplating dinner."

Diesel grinned down at me. "I like a hungry woman. Makes life easy. I don't have to work hard to satisfy her."

"Are we talking about food?"

"Yeah, that too." He motioned to two bags on the counter. "I got Chinese. Not especially authentic but should be okay."

I pulled the cartons out of the bag. Kung pao chicken, fried rice, steamed dumplings, some kind of glutinous vegetable mix.

"This is great," I said. "Thank you."

The smile was still in place. "How grateful are you?"

"Grateful enough to let you stay one more night."

Diesel got a couple forks out of the silverware drawer and handed one to me. "That's a start."

We dumped the food out onto a common plate and dug in.

"How's the force feeling today?" I asked.

"It's not good."

"What does that mean?"

"It means I've got a cramp in my ass that won't go away."

"Usually that means your cousin Wulf is in town."

"I haven't seen him, but it's possible."

"I'm going to assume he's not the source of the ass cramp."

"Not at this moment." Diesel got a beer out of the fridge. "I guess that could change."

Diesel's cousin Wulf is a dark, mysterious guy with seemingly magical abilities. Diesel regards him as all smoke and mirrors, but I'm not sure. I met him once, briefly, and I couldn't determine if he was very good or very evil.

"So, are you going to tell me the source of your ass cramp?" I asked Diesel.

"No."

"It wouldn't be zombies, would it?"

"Not likely. Personally, I think they get a bad rap."

"I hear they like brains."

"That's the rumor." He looked down at the food plate. "Are you going to eat that last dumpling?"

"No. I'm full."

My phone buzzed with a text message from my mom. *Your grandmother needs a ride to the viewing, and I'm holding you responsible if she shoots someone, gets arrested, or tries to take a selfie with the deceased.*

Stick a fork in my eye, I thought. It would be less painful than going to the viewing with Grandma.

"I don't suppose you brought any dessert?" I asked Diesel.

"Dessert is the work of the devil."

"I'm unhappy. I *need* dessert."

"I have something better than dessert. Happiness guaranteed."

"Gonna pass on that."

"You'll come around," Diesel said.

I had a fear that he was right. I had limitations on my ability to resist temptation.

I washed my fork and put it in the dish drain. "I have to change my clothes. I'm taking Grandma to a viewing tonight."

"Emily Molinowski," Diesel said.

I raised an eyebrow.

Diesel tossed the empty food cartons into the garbage. "Lucky guess."

I decided on a slim knee-length skirt, sleeveless scoop-neck sweater with a matching cardigan, and ballet flats. Heels would have been sexier, but I wasn't going for sexy. I was going for comfy.

Diesel was stretched out on the couch when I walked into the living room.

"And you're doing what?" I asked him.

"Communicating."

I stared at him for a long moment. "You're a strange man."

"Yeah," he said. "I'm special."

TEN

GRANDMA WAS WAITING at the door when I drove up to my parents' house. She called goodbye to my mom and trotted out to my Lexus.

"This is going to be something," she said, buckling in. "I heard they did a real good job at the funeral home, and you can't hardly see where they attached the head. That's sort of disappointing, but I guess it's comforting to the family of the deceased."

"Mom said no selfies with Emily."

"Your mom is a wet blanket. How did she get to be so old?"

"I think it was living with us."

"I guess someone has to be the adult," Grandma said. "I'm glad it's not me. Been there. Done that."

The lot next to the funeral home was already full when I pulled in, and cars were lined up at the curb for blocks. People were milling around on the sidewalk, waiting for the doors to open.

"This is worse than I thought," Grandma said. "It's like the whole state of New Jersey showed up."

I dropped Grandma in front of the funeral home and went off in search of a place to park. By the time I parked and walked back, the doors were open and everyone was filing into the building. I didn't see Grandma. No surprise. She would have fought her way to the front of the line and been one of the first inside.

I was content to be one of the last. I hated the crush of mourners, the smell of funeral flowers, and the claustrophobic "Slumber Room" without windows where the recently passed resided and people spoke in hushed voices.

I got a text from Grandma that said she was saving a seat for me in the second row, and I texted back that I preferred to stand.

I maneuvered myself through the lobby and into the Slumber Room, where I plastered myself against the back wall, not far from the door. I could see everyone coming and going, and I was within striking distance if Johnny showed up.

I was dividing my attention between the line that was very slowly moving past Emily, the mob that was trying to squeeze into the room, and Grandma. If Grandma caused a scene and it got back to my mom, I'd be cut off from pineapple upside-down cake for the rest of my life.

The viewing hours were seven o'clock to nine o'clock. At eight o'clock I saw Diesel enter the room. He nodded to me, looked around, and left. He didn't seem to be interested in Emily, and he didn't wander over to say hello to me, so I supposed the drop-in might be work related.

My understanding is that Diesel has a job that is a little like mine. He works for a mysterious private organization, and he tracks down organization members who abuse their power. I know nothing beyond this, but I'm pretty sure he doesn't kill people.

Johnny Chucci's mother was sitting in the middle of the viewing room. Chucci's sister, Penny, was with her. I didn't see any of the Chucci men. Johnny's brother Earl was my age. We went through school together, but he was never in any of my classes, and we never hung out. The second brother, Little Pinkie, I only knew in passing. His given name is George but everyone calls him Little Pinkie because he has a stump for a little finger on his left hand.

A woman approached the casket, looked down at Emily, and fainted. She was the third woman to faint so far. My guess is that the head hadn't gone on perfectly.

Grandma abandoned her seat at eight-thirty and made her way to the lobby. This was standard procedure for her at this point in time. Her lady friends would be collecting around the refreshment table. They'd exchange gossip, critique the appearance of the deceased, and stuff cookies into their purses.

I joined Grandma a couple minutes before closing.

"You should have come out earlier," Grandma said. "All the good cookies are gone."

"Did you learn anything interesting?"

"A couple people have seen Johnny. Myrna Zuck ran into

him at the Italian bakery. He was buying a rye bread. And Florence Minkowski saw him at Cluck-in-a-Bucket. No one knows where he's staying. I asked the mother and sister about him, and they grabbed the last two Oreos and rushed off."

Lights dimmed as a signal that the viewing was over.

"It was a good viewing but not great," Grandma said. "It would have been better if the zombie had taken Harold Kucher's brain. Harold's the exalted ruler of the Benevolent and Protective Order of Elks. There would have been a big ceremony for him. All the Elks would have been here wearing their sashes and hats and medals. As it was, we just had some fainters."

Grandma and I followed the crowd to the door, where the funeral director was wishing everyone a good night.

"It was pretty good work, considering the problem you must have had fixing the head back on," Grandma told the funeral director.

The funeral director nodded in agreement. "We try our best."

"I couldn't help notice it was screwed on a little crooked," Grandma said.

The funeral director squelched a grimace, and I moved Grandma through the door and down the stairs.

"You must have had a hard time finding a place to park," Grandma said. "There's cars all up and down the street."

"I cheated and parked in the driveway for the funeral home garages. We can take a shortcut through the parking lot."

The parking lot ran the length of one side of the funeral home. The garages were to the rear, shielded from view by a hedge and some chunky shrubs. We walked through the lot and skirted around the hedge. The funeral director's car was parked by the building's rear exit. The hearses and flower cars were out of sight in the garage. The area was lit by an overhead flood. The Lexus was discreetly parked in a shaded area on the edge of the drive.

We approached the car and something rustled in the bushes. My first thought was animal. My second thought was funeral director.

Grandma hauled her gun out of her purse and two-handed it in front of her. "Who's there?" she said. "I've got a gun so you better be careful."

There was more rustling. Something gave a guttural grunt, and for a split second I thought I saw the outline of a man. He was in dark shadow. He was there, and then he was gone.

"Do you smell that?" Grandma asked. "That's the stink of a zombie."

"Are you sure it's not the dumpster?"

"Two entirely different stinks," Grandma said. "There was a zombie prowling around out here. No doubt he was looking for a brain to eat, and I scared him away."

"No doubt."

"We should tell the funeral director," Grandma said.

"That might not be a good idea," I said, opening the car door for Grandma. "We're not supposed to be parked back here." Not to mention, most sane people don't entirely believe in zombies.

"I forgot about that. I guess we should keep quiet, but I'm going to feel real bad if he comes back and eats someone's brain."

. . .

I turned Grandma over to my mom and went home to a quiet apartment. Rex was running on his wheel. Diesel was off, doing his Diesel thing. No zombies lurking in my kitchen. Ranger's car was safely parked in the lot behind my building. It was all good.

I poured myself a glass of wine, tucked a box of Froot Loops under my arm, and settled in front of the television. I watched three recorded episodes of *The Mind of a Chef* and one episode of *Barnwood Builders*. I don't cook and I don't have any plans to build a barn, but I'm hooked on the shows.

Before heading to bed, I threw the deadbolt and put the security chain in place on my apartment door. I knew it wouldn't stop Diesel from getting in, but it might make it more of a challenge.

I was dragged out of sleep by a warm body moving next to me. I looked at my bedside clock. Four in the morning. An arm curled around me and drew me closer to the body. Diesel was back.

"Are you asleep?" he asked.

"Yes," I said.

"Any chance you'll wake up?"

"Not any time soon."

His hand strayed toward my breast. "Let me know if you change your mind."

I rolled over onto my stomach. "You'll be the first to know. And don't even think about what you're thinking about."

I was doing my best to sound authoritative and off-limits, but I was thinking he felt good next to me. And then I was thinking that was horrible and wrong. And that was followed by the possibility that I might not care if it was wrong. And then I realized he'd fallen asleep.

Men! *Ugh*.

ELEVEN

I WOKE UP in a vicious mood. Ignoring my black eye, I stomped off to the bathroom, took a shower, pulled my hair into a ponytail, swiped on some mascara, got dressed in my usual uniform, and stomped back to the bed where Diesel was sleeping.

"Hey!" I yelled.

"What?" Diesel asked without opening his eyes.

"I'm leaving."

"Are you naked?"

"No."

"Did you make breakfast for me?"

"No."

Silence. Even breathing. Eyes closed.

"Hey!" I yelled again. "Are you sleeping?"

He opened his eyes. "Not anymore. And the 'Hey' thing is getting old."

"Just checking."

"You have a mean streak," Diesel said. "You ever think about meditation? Chamomile tea?"

"You ever think about leaving?"

"Not in the last ten minutes."

I was doomed. If he stayed long enough, my hormones would eventually disconnect my brain, and I'd be on him like white on rice. Bad enough I was in jeopardy of having an *arrangement* with Ranger, I now had Mr. Big, Hot, and Blond tempting me toward total slutdom.

"Here's the thing," I said. "I'm in a relationship and . . ."

His eyes were closed again. Damn! He was asleep.

I blew out a sigh and took one last look. He was beyond annoying when he was awake, and deliciously adorable when he was asleep.

. . .

I called Morelli on my way to the office and got his voicemail. "Just checking in," I told him. "Hope everything's good."

That got a grimace out of me. How good could it be? The man was collecting heads without brains.

I stopped at Dunkin' Donuts and got coffee, a breakfast sandwich, and a dozen donuts. Probably overkill, but I was looking to seriously increase my endorphin production.

Connie looked up when I walked in. I dumped my messenger bag on the couch, set the box of donuts on her desk, and tucked into the breakfast sandwich.

"What's new?" I asked.

"Vinnie phoned in and was on a rant about Zero Slick. Apparently, you made national news. Vinnie said he was watching television, and he saw Slick hit you with a sign. He wants to know why you didn't bring him in."

I pointed to my eye, which was now a dark green with touches of navy and magenta. "Hit and run. By the time my head cleared Slick was gone. Where is Vinnie?"

"He's at a conference in Atlanta."

Lula shuffled into the office. She looked like someone set off a bomb in her head and her hair exploded. She was wearing red sneakers, gray sweatpants, and a pink T-shirt with a coffee stain down the front of it.

"God bless someone, on account of I see a box of donuts on the desk," Lula said. "Tell me there's still donuts left in that box."

"Tough night?" Connie asked.

"The worst. Dogs barking and cats howling. Then there was people yelling at the dogs and cats to shut up. Then there were sirens and flashy lights in my window. Not that any of this is unusual in my neighborhood. I've grown skills that help me to ignore these distractions. It's that none of my skills helped last night. I finally gave up trying to sleep somewhere around five in the morning. I got dressed and went out to see what the fuss was about. I thought maybe I would take a jog around the block. I've been planning on taking up exercise."

Lula crammed a donut into her mouth and selected a second. "Healthy body, healthy mind. That's what I'm all about. Who picked these donuts out? There's only two of them Boston Kreme. I mean, I'm in a donut emergency. I need at least four Boston Kremes. And I need coffee."

"Looks like you already had coffee," Connie said.

Lula looked down at herself. "This isn't my coffee. I was out in front of my house, and I was thinking about going for a walk or a run or something, and I bumped into a cop. The place was crawling with them. This is his coffee."

"What was the problem?" I asked. "Why were the police there?"

"I don't know," Lula said. "After I got the coffee spilled on me I went back inside and fell asleep on the couch. I woke up a couple hours later and there were still dogs barking and cop cars with their stupid radios squawking, so I came here to get some quiet." She ate two more donuts and went to the coffee machine at the back of the room. "I should move out of that neighborhood, but I like my apartment. It's got a big closet." She returned with coffee and ate another donut.

"I just got off the phone with Maureen Segal," Connie said to Lula. "She was on police dispatch last night. She said your next-door neighbor let his dog out to do his business around midnight, and the dog found a body in the bushes."

"Nothing new about that," Lula said.

"Yes, but the body didn't have a head."

I suppose this explained why I hadn't heard back from Morelli.

Lula's eyes opened wide. "Get the heck out! I should have known. It's the zombies. That's why I couldn't sleep. I got ESP for zombies. I got zombie radar. I thought I smelled something too. It was like carnations and outhouse." She looked into the donut box. "What do you think this is with the pink icing? Strawberry? Cherry? Anybody mind if I eat it?"

Connie and I shook our heads. We didn't mind. After the carnation and outhouse sensory message the pink donut wasn't doing it for me.

"I need to roll," I said to Lula and Connie. "I have a plan."

It wasn't a good plan, but it was the best I could come up with, and it would look like I was working.

"What's your plan?" Lula asked. "I might need to join you."

"I'm going to check on Ethel, then I'm going to cruise around Slick's burned-out building and maybe pay another visit to his parents. Then I'm going to have lunch with Grandma to see if she's got any more information on Johnny Chucci."

"I like that plan," Lula said. "I especially like the lunch part."

We went to my car, and Lula looked in the back seat.

"Do you have food for Ethel?" Lula asked. "I don't see no food."

I ran back into the office and returned with the donut box. I handed it to Lula and got behind the wheel.

"I might need to eat one more of these before we give them to Ethel," Lula said.

By the time we got to Ethel there were only two donuts left in the box. I unlocked the door to the double-wide and looked in. Ethel was curled on the dinette table. I said hello and told her hopefully Diggery would be home soon. I left the box on the floor just inside the door, locked up, and went back to my car.

"How'd that go?" Lula asked.

"Okay. Ethel was on the table. Nothing looked out of the ordinary."

I drove to the building Slick burned down and made a slow pass around the block. The crime scene tape had been taken down, and it looked like the neighborhood had normalized. There were some street people sitting out in the morning sun. I glanced at Lula and decided she would have more luck talking to the street people than I would. She sort of looked like one of them today.

"I'm going to drop you off," I told Lula. "Ask the locals about Slick. I'll continue to drive and explore the area, and I'll pick you up in a half hour."

"No problemo. Now that I'm all sugared up I'm ready to go. Lula is my name, and undercover is my game."

I gave her double thumbs-up and rolled away. I methodically worked a nine-block grid, driving the streets. I looked for Slick, and I looked for abandoned buildings.

Lula was waiting on the corner for me when I circled back to her.

"This was an unsatisfying experience," she said. "Those street people are rude. They said I was a disgrace to street people on account of I have a coffee stain."

"Did you get any information on Slick?"

"Yeah. He stops around to get lunch sometimes. No one's seen him lately. They all think he's a genius. Like he has ideas about how to be a billionaire. One of them was to be a drug lord. So how did that turn out?"

"You have a new stain on your shirt."

Lula looked down at herself. "One of the volunteers gave me some soup. It was in a Styrofoam cup with a plastic spoon, and it wasn't all that easy to get at."

"Not like eating a donut."

"Not nearly. Did you get anything on your drive-around?"

"No. Not a lot of people out at this time of the morning, and I didn't see any vacant buildings that could be used to cook drugs."

"From what I heard today, Slick probably gave up on the drug empire. Sounded to me like he has a short attention span. Like he jumps around from one scheme to the next."

"Do we have a clue about his new scheme?"

"They said he was talking about being a movie star. And he was also thinking about going to Tuscany and starting a vineyard."

"Oh boy."

"Yeah, it's a little out there, but you gotta respect a man who dreams big."

"You smell like minestrone," I said to Lula.

"It's my shirt. The minestrone was the homeless soup of the day. I wouldn't mind a short stop at my apartment, so I could beautify myself."

I thought that was an excellent idea, and there was a chance that Morelli would still be at the crime scene.

Lula lived in a lavender and pink two-story frame house that had been converted into four apartments. The owner of the house lived on the ground floor. Lula lived on the second floor. And a crazy woman lived in the attic. The street was narrow and lined with trees. The residents were ethnically mixed and uniformly straddling the poverty line. It was a nice street that was too close to some very bad, gang-infested streets.

I left downtown, drove to Lula's neighborhood, and took the alley that ran past the back of Lula's apartment. Lula had a dedicated parking spot that I was able to slide into. The rest of the street and alley space was clogged with police vehicles, satellite TV trucks, and clumps of curious bystanders. Some of the bystanders were dressed like zombies.

Lula disappeared inside her house, and I went in search of Morelli. I found him on the sidewalk, in front of the CSI van, standing back on his heels, looking lost in thought.

"What's going on?" I asked him.

"This is turning into a freak show."

"Are you still in charge?"

"No one's in charge," Morelli said. "The state is here. The feds are here. Zombie National Chapter 103 is here."

"Those are the guys in rags?"

"Yeah, they're waiting for the apocalypse."

"Nice. What are *you* waiting for?"

"Inspiration," Morelli said. "The headless bodies are stacking up like cordwood, and I'm not making any progress."

"Have you identified the guy in the bushes?"

"Yes. He was stolen from the funeral home on Stark Street."

"Do you have . . . *all* of him?"

"No. The state guys are talking about bringing in a clairvoyant."

"Do you think that will help?"

"I stopped thinking a couple hours ago."

The zombie chapter had a boom box going. They were playing the "Monster Mash" and marching around stiff-legged with their arms stretched out in front of them.

"This is a little carny," I said to Morelli.

"This is nothing. There are food trucks and T-shirt vendors on the next block."

Lula approached us. She had changed into a short purple metallic wig, a black low-cut sweater that barely contained *the girls,* and black Pilates pants that fit her like skin.

"Just look at this," Lula said, spreading her arms wide, taking the scene in. "This is what I'm talking about. Here's people changing something bad into something rad. It's like a wake with a lot of liquor and meatballs. This could set Trenton back on the map. Not everywhere you got a zombie fest going on."

"This is a murder scene," I said.

"Technically it's not a murder scene," Morelli said.

"Yeah, and technically these aren't real zombies," Lula said. "These here are *fun* zombies."

I didn't think they looked all that much fun. I thought they were creepy.

"Maybe these *fun* zombies are all actually nuts and like to eat brains," I said.

Morelli looked over at them. "We thought of that. We have them all on record. Names, addresses, photos and video."

I followed Morelli's line of sight and studied the zombies. "I don't suppose Zero Slick happens to be with them?"

"No. For what it's worth we don't have him in the zombie registry."

"You got a zombie registry?" Lula asked. "That sounds wrong. You better be careful or you'll get accused of zombie harassment."

"Been there, done that," Morelli said.

"Gotta go," I said. "Stuff to do."

TWELVE

LULA AND I walked to the back of her apartment building and got into the Lexus.

"I wouldn't mind taking a look at the street with the food trucks and T-shirts," Lula said. "I might want a commemorative T-shirt."

I drove around the block, found the food truck street, and cruised the length of it. It was slow going because it was packed with people. They were buying ice cream in waffle cones, cotton candy, sausage sandwiches, zombie glow sticks, zombie T-shirts, and zombie ball caps. A guy dressed in zombie rags was playing the accordion. A sign advertised valet parking.

"I'm thinking if you use valet parking here you're not likely to get your car back," Lula said.

"Do you need to buy something?" I asked her.

"Not bad enough to stand in line for it. Where'd all these people come from? Why aren't they working?"

I cut across town and took Klockner to Majestic Mews. I parked a short distance from the Krakowski apartment and settled in.

"How long are we going to sit here?" Lula asked.

"Until lunch."

"In that case, I'm putting my seat back and taking a nap. As you know, I didn't have an ideal night."

A little after eleven o'clock, Marie Krakowski exited her apartment and walked to a silver Nissan Sentra. She was carrying a bulging cloth grocery bag and a small cooler chest. Bingo. Dollars to donuts she was taking lunch to her son.

"We're on the move," I said to Lula. "Raise your seat."

Marie pulled out of the lot, and I followed at a distance. She left Hamilton Township and took Olden Avenue to Morley Street.

"Oh crap," Lula said. "She's going to the cemetery. She's taking lunch to the zombies. You said she has a cooler. Maybe she's got a head in it."

"Marie Krakowski doesn't impress me as being a zombie chaser. She's a mom, and I'm pretty sure she's feeding her son."

"Yeah, but he could be a zombie by now if he's in the zombie cemetery."

The cemetery on Morley Street was small as far as cemeteries go. It was attached to a nondenominational church that was also small. Both were very old, dating back to the Revolution.

Marie parked in the church parking lot and took her cooler and grocery bag through the wrought iron gate that led to the cemetery.

"Now what?" Lula said.

"We wait. I don't want to create a scene when the mother is there."

"That's real nice of you."

It had nothing to do with being nice. Marie Krakowski was an additional complication. One more person to worry about. She could be carrying a gun in the cooler. Never underestimate a protective mother.

She was in the cemetery for twenty minutes. When she returned to her car she was empty-handed. I waited for her to leave the parking lot and then I entered the cemetery.

"Stay here at the gate," I told Lula. "If he takes off on me, he'll run this way and you can stop him."

"No problem," Lula said, "but we should have a code word if that happens, so I'm ready."

"How about if I yell out '*Stop him!*'"

"Yeah, that'll work. And I'm getting my gun ready, so if any zombies show up I can shoot them in the head."

I followed the path from the gate toward the heart of the cemetery. Most of the headstones here were old and weather beaten, names and dates no longer readable. The newer graves were located at the far end, but they were few and far between. The plots had been used for generations, and space was scarce.

I found Zero Slick sitting with his back to a tombstone, dousing a ham sandwich with Tabasco sauce. He looked up when I approached, but he didn't seem alarmed.

"So?" I asked.

"So, what?"

"What are you doing here?"

"Eating lunch. Go away."

"I feel like there's a story here," I said to Slick.

"It's none of your business."

"Not true," I said. "I'm supposed to capture you. Right now, everything you do is my business."

"Capturing me won't do anybody any good."

"It'll be good for me. I get money when I bring you in."

"A pittance compared to what I'm going to make. Two months from now I'll be world-famous, and you'll still be nothing."

"How so?"

"I'm not telling you."

"Here's the deal. I'm going to cuff you and drive you back to the police station. Court is in session right now so you'll be able to get bonded out again, and you'll be free to come back to this cemetery in a couple hours."

"No way. I'm not leaving the cemetery. I have important work to do here."

I reached for him, and he jumped away. I pulled my cuffs and stun gun out, and he took off, running for the gate. I yelled "Stop him!" and a couple seconds later I heard *ooof* and *wump*. By the time I got to Lula, she was sitting on Slick, and he was struggling to breathe.

I cuffed him, and Lula and I hauled him to his feet.

"Another minute and I would have been dead," Slick said, sucking air. "How much do you weigh? Three hundred pounds? You need some serious portion control. You probably eat enough every day to feed half of the people who are starving in Burundi."

"Look who's talking," Lula said. "Mr. Pudgy Wudgy."

"I'll make a deal," Slick said. "If you let me stay here, I'll let you buy in to my project."

"No," I said.

"You have to let me stay!" Slick said. "This could be my big break."

"You'll only be gone for a couple hours," I told him.

"I'll be gone forever. No one's going to bond me out this time. My parents aren't going to bond me out again. And I have no one else."

"Not my problem," I said.

"He's got my curiosity," Lula said. "I want to know about the big break. I'm always on the lookout for a big break."

"It's the zombies," Slick said. "I found the portal. There's only one place in this whole cemetery where the earth has been disturbed."

"You aren't gonna turn into a zombie, are you?" Lula asked. "I have to tell you that's not a big break. Those zombies are unattractive."

"I'm going to film them," Slick said. "I'm going to make a zombie documentary. It's genius, right? Nobody's done it."

"Because there really aren't zombies?" I asked.

"Don't pay attention to her," Lula said to Slick. "She's one of them disbelievers. I think this has potential. How are you gonna do this?"

"I'm going to sit here and wait until the zombies show up. I figure they might be coming and going. Like this is home base. And then when they show up I'm going to film them."

"You got equipment?" Lula asked.

"I have a GoPro that has infrared filming, and I have my cellphone."

"I might know where you can get some professional stuff," Lula said. "As I see it, your big problem is stopping the zombies from eating your brain."

"So far, they're only taking brains from people who are already dead, so I think I'm safe as long as I'm alive."

Lula nodded. "I can see you thought this through."

"It's a chance of a lifetime," Slick said. "I'd be willing to give you a credit if you could get me better equipment. I could list you as an assistant or a grip or something."

"My name would have to be in a prominent place," Lula said. "I'd need to get a producer credit. And what about the filming? Would we get to be seen with the zombies?"

"I hadn't thought about it, but sure, we could do that."

"It would enhance our prospects for future film roles," Lula said. "It could lead to us being movie stars."

Slick was visibly excited. His eyes were wide and his face was flushed. "Exactly! That's been my plan all along."

"Okay, it's decided," Lula said. "Let's do it."

I raised my hand. "Hello? Have we forgotten something? This man is a felon. We're supposed to be apprehending him."

"Yeah, but I don't see where there's such a rush," Lula said. "We got a mission. It could be critical that we document the zombies."

I rolled my eyes and thunked the heel of my hand against my forehead. *"Unh!"*

"I gotta get back to my post," Slick said. "I don't want any zombies sneaking into the portal without getting their picture taken."

"And I gotta go to the projects and find my camera friend," Lula said.

Lula hustled off to the parking lot, and I followed after her.

"We have to find Cheap Slim," Lula said. "He's my electronics source these days."

I knew about Cheap Slim. He sold cameras, smartphones, watches, and laptops out of the trunk of his 1998 Cadillac Eldorado. Best not to ask about the source of his goods.

"You're going to buy a camera to film something that doesn't exist," I said to Lula.

"Well, *something* came out of the cemetery and followed Diggery home," Lula said. "And *something*'s collecting brains."

She had a point. So maybe putting Slick in the cemetery with a camera wasn't such a bad idea.

"It's almost noon," I said. "I called my mom a while ago and told her we'd be around for lunch. After lunch we can look for Cheap Slim."

"Sounds good. Now that I think about it, I might even have a camera at my apartment. It was left over from when I did the bungee jumping demo."

THIRTEEN

"YOU PICKED A good day to come for lunch," Grandma told Lula. "We got leftover meatloaf, fresh bakery bread, and coleslaw. And I got a new picture of my honey."

"Is this the guy who looks like George Hamilton?" Lula asked.

"Yep. This is a picture of him on his scooter."

Lula and I looked at the photo on Grandma's cellphone.

"He's almost as dark as me," Lula said. "He spends some serious time in the sun."

"Well, he's in Florida and that's the way it is. I'm told everyone looks like this in Florida," Grandma said. "I might have to go to a tanning salon before I visit him."

"You are *not* visiting him," my mother said.

Lula and I took a seat at the kitchen table. I made a meatloaf sandwich and helped myself to the coleslaw.

"Have you heard anything new about Johnny Chucci?" I asked Grandma.

"I got a load of information about Johnny," Grandma said. "He came back because he had a dream about his ex-wife, and he decided he was still in love with her. He tried to go visit her, and she hit him on the head with a fry pan, and he had to go to the emergency room. Twelve stitches. Went home and had another dream. This time God told him he had to try again. He's afraid to go back, so he's been sending her stuff. Flowers and pizza and love notes. So far as I know, the ex-wife wants nothing to do with him."

"That's pathetic," Lula said. "If someone sent me pizza I'd have to reconsider my feelings for him."

Grandma forked in some meatloaf. "Word is that he even forgives her for killing his dog with the chicken bone."

"He sounds like a nice man," Lula said. "A real romantic. It's a shame we gotta haul his ass back to jail, but I guess that's life, right?"

"Do you know where he's staying?" I asked Grandma. "Where's home these days?"

"He was staying with his brother Earl, but that got old for Earl's wife," Grandma said. "Then he moved in with his brother Little Pinkie, and he might still be there. And that's all I know except that Johnny doesn't look so good these days, and he might be a zombie."

Lula sat forward in her seat. "Get out! Is that for real?"

"Well, he's not raggedy, but his eyes are sort of sunken in like zombie eyes. I guess he could just be anemic, but people are talking."

"What's he smell like?" Lula asked. "Did anybody smell him?"

"I haven't heard anything about his smell," Grandma said.

My mother brought half a chocolate cake to the table. "For goodness' sakes, the man got hit in the head with a fry pan. He's probably got a headache." She knifed into the cake and put a slab onto a plate. "Who wants dessert?"

We all wanted dessert.

. . .

We finished lunch and pushed back from the table.

"I'd offer to help you take down Johnny," Grandma said, "but I got an appointment at the hair salon. I have to keep up appearances in case my honey decides to visit me or vice versa."

My mother still had the cake knife on the table. She was looking like she wanted to plunge it into her heart and end it all, so I removed the knife from the table, washed it, dried it, and put it back in the knife drawer.

"Great lunch, Mrs. P.," Lula said. "You sure know how to put out a spread."

I gave my mom a hug. "Thanks for the lunch. Don't worry about Grandma."

"I'll never forgive your grandfather for dying," my mother said. "God bless his soul."

. . .

Lula and I drove four blocks and parked across the street from Little Pinkie Chucci's house.

"It doesn't say anything about him in the file," Lula said. "Is he married?"

"He's married to a guy named Butch. They both work at the gym on Center Street. Butch is a physical therapist, and Little Pinkie is a trainer."

We crossed the street, and I rang Little Pinkie's doorbell. No one answered, but there was a lot of barking on the other side of the door. I rang the bell a second time, and the barking continued.

"I'm guessing that Little Pinkie and Butch are at work, and Johnny isn't here either," I said. "If someone was home they would have attempted to stop the barking."

Lula was already creeping around the house, looking in the windows.

"The dog that's making all that noise is about three pounds. It's one of those Chihuahua dogs," Lula said. "I can see the little ankle biter looking up at me."

I moved next to Lula, checked out the dog, and continued walking. I was able to see the kitchen from the back door window. Everything was neat and clean. Two cereal bowls and two juice glasses in the dish drain. No indication that a third person was living in the house.

"No sign of Mr. Underpants," Lula said. "Now what?"

"Now we go to the gym to talk to Little Pinkie."

"Okay, but don't forget about Slick. I promised him a camera."

"It's on my list."

Ethel was also on my list. I didn't think two donuts was going to hold her, and the last thing I wanted was for her to be ravenously hungry when I opened Diggery's door.

The Center Street gym was a large, blocky freestanding building with statues of Greek gods by the front door. We found Little Pinkie in the free-weights area. I hadn't seen him in years, but he was as I remembered. Over-muscled and over-tattooed. Dark hair slicked back. Missing a finger.

He recognized me too, and he guessed why I was there.

"Johnny was crashing at my house, but it didn't work," Little Pinkie said. "Killer hated him."

"Killer?" I asked.

"My dog."

"The Chihuahua?"

"Yeah. It was unpleasant, so Johnny moved out."

"Do you know where he went?"

"Sure, but I'm not telling you. That would be ratting on my brother."

"Yeah, but he's a felon," Lula said. "And besides that, he's a goofball. He robbed a jewelry store wearing a pair of tighty-whities on his head."

"He might have been 'shroomed up, but he's clean now," Little Pinkie said. "He's trying to get his life together."

"He could get it together in prison," Lula said. "They got dumbbells there. He could come out looking like you."

"Something to think about," Little Pinkie said, "but I'm not telling you where he is."

We left the gym and went to Lula's apartment to get the camera. I drove her to the cemetery, but she wouldn't go beyond the gate.

"You've got to take the camera to him," Lula said. "I don't like cemeteries, and I don't like zombies. And the thing is, I've got the feeling that I'm one of those people who attracts zombies. And now that we're here I'm going creepy-crawly."

"I thought you were all into this. You wanted to be filmed with the zombies."

"I'm rethinking that part of it. I could be interviewed at some other location, and they could edit me in. They do that stuff all the time."

I rolled my eyes and blew out a sigh. It wasn't a spectacular eye roll. I didn't really have my heart in it. Truth is, I was getting weary of the zombie routine. I took the camera and walked it back to Slick. He was sitting with his back to a tree, and he was writing in a journal.

"What are you writing?" I asked him.

"A book. I'm going to send it to Oprah when I'm done."

"You have big plans."

"I'm short. I have to think tall."

I nodded acknowledgment. It was an admirable philosophy. It would be even better if he threw some common sense into the tall thinking.

"I don't suppose you've spotted any zombies," I said.

"Not yet. I'm hoping for some good activity tonight."

I handed the camera to him. "This is from Lula. It didn't come with an instruction book, but hopefully you can figure it out." I gave him my card. "Call me if you see any zombies, or if you get tired of sitting here and want to get carted off to jail."

"I don't suppose you have any weed on you?"

"Nope. No weed."

I left him sitting under the tree, and I returned to Lula.

"How's he doing?" she asked.

"He's okay."

"He see any zombies yet?"

"Nope. No zombies."

"Well, they're out there, sneaking around. I can feel them watching me. And I think they might be sending me mental messages."

"What are they saying?"

"They're saying . . . brains, brains, brains."

I did a 360-degree scan. I didn't see any zombies, and I wasn't getting any mental messages.

"I need to get more food for Ethel," I said to Lula. "Something inexpensive."

"How inexpensive are you thinking? Roadkill? Dumpster pickings?"

"More like almost expired rotisserie chicken."

"That's still going to add up to money. If you could find a woodchuck on the side of the road it would last Ethel a couple days."

"Are you going to pick it up?"

"Hell, no. You're the one who promised to take care of Ethel. I'm not picking up no dead woodchuck."

I pulled into a Shop and Bag and got six rotisserie chickens. Four for Ethel, one for me, and one for Lula.

"Those chickens smell delicious," Lula said. "I'm having a feast tonight. I'm going to stop at the deli on my way home and get some potato salad and a banana cream pie."

After buying all those chickens, banana cream pie would not

fit into my budget. Roadkill for Ethel was looking more attractive.

I turned onto Broad, and saw Johnny Chucci come out of the hardware store and walk down the street.

"That's him!" I said. "That's Johnny Chucci in the blue shirt and jeans."

I pulled to the side of the road and parked at a bus stop. Lula and I got out of the car, crossed the street, and ran after Chucci. He got into a silver Honda and drove away before we got to him. Lula and I ran back to my car and took off after him. He was in sight, with two cars between us. He turned off Broad and onto Liberty. He was heading into the Burg.

"When I get close enough I want you to get his plate," I said to Lula. "Just in case we lose him."

"I'm on it."

I closed the distance between us, and Chucci suddenly turned into an alley and sped up.

"He's onto us," Lula said.

I was on his bumper. Chucci clipped a garbage can, and it flipped up and smashed into the side of the Lexus.

"Keep going," Lula said. "That didn't hardly do any damage." She had her gun out and her window rolled down. "You want me to shoot him?" she asked. "I could shoot out his tires."

Lula couldn't hit the broad side of a barn if she was two feet away. She is the worst shot of anyone I know.

"No!" I said. "No shooting."

Chucci made a hard left onto Myrtle Street and an immediate right into another alley. I stayed with him until he suddenly turned left into a backyard, raced between two houses, and came out on Clifton. I didn't react fast enough to follow him through the yard. By the time I got to Clifton he was gone.

I drove around the Burg, looking for the silver Honda, while Lula called the plate in to Connie.

"Connie says the car belongs to Little Pinkie."

I drove past Little Pinkie's house. Car wasn't there. I drove past the gym. Car wasn't there either.

I gave up searching for Johnny and went to feed Ethel. The sky was overcast, and by the time we reached Diggery's road, the sun was hidden behind the trees.

"It's not nighttime," Lula said, "but it's dark enough back here in the woods that it's spooky."

I thought it was spooky in full daylight. It was like being in a second-rate goblin forest. It wouldn't surprise me to find flying demon monkeys living in one of the yurts.

I parked in Diggery's front yard, let myself into the double-wide, and arranged the chickens on the small kitchen table. I heard the whisper of a sound from the bedroom, and a chill ran down my spine. Ethel was on the move. Her head poked into the hallway, and at the same time Lula barreled through the front door and slammed it shut.

"They're out there. The zombies are coming to get me. I got out of the car for a minute to stretch my legs, and I saw them. They were heading for the car, so I ran in here."

I looked out the window. I didn't see any zombies.

"I don't even have my gun," Lula said. "I left my purse in the car."

"I don't see them," I said. "You must have scared them away."

"Maybe they went invisible. Crack the window and see if you can smell them."

"I can't smell anything but rotisserie chicken," I said.

Lula caught sight of Ethel oozing closer, hunting down dinner.

"Holy hell!" Lula said. "I'm caught between a giant snake and the zombies. I gotta get out of here. Give me one of those chickens."

"What are you going to do with it?"

"I'm gonna give it to the zombies. They can have chicken brain."

"These are supermarket chickens," I said. "They don't have heads."

"Say what?"

"Look at them. No head. No brain. Didn't you ever notice that supermarket chickens don't have a head?"

"I never thought about it. Maybe the zombies won't notice."

"Of course, they'll notice," I said. "These are rotisserie chickens."

Ethel was almost entirely in the hall, looking bigger in the small space than when she was curled in the tree.

"That's the biggest freaking snake I've ever seen," Lula said. "I'm gonna get diarrhea."

"That would be bad," I told her. "The bathroom is on the other side of Ethel."

Lula was dancing around, waving her arms in the air. "I got to get out of here. I got to get out of here."

I opened the front door, and Lula rushed through it and down the makeshift stairs. I stepped out of the double-wide, locked the door, and came up behind her. She was standing dead still in the middle of the yard. Her eyes were wide, and her mouth was open. No sounds were coming out of Lula, but there were low, guttural moans coming out of the woods surrounding us.

"W-w-what the hell is that?" Lula whispered, pointing to the patch of scrubby bushes beyond the car.

The area was in deep shadow, but I saw two pairs of red eyes and what appeared to be two human forms.

"Get in the car," I whispered.

"W-w-what?"

"GET IN THE CAR!"

I gave her a shove, and we jumped into the car. I roared out of the yard and down the road. I followed a curve in the road, and something sprang out of the woods at us and bounced off my front right quarter panel. I hit the brake, jerking to a stop.

"What was that?" I asked Lula.

"It was a zombie! Lordy, lordy, you ran over one of the zombies. Okay, so they're already dead, but I'm guessing they aren't gonna be happy about this. Nobody likes getting run over."

"It was an accident."

"Yeah, but you ran over him all the same. You smacked right into him!"

I turned in my seat and looked at the road behind us. I couldn't see anything. I got out of the car and looked around.

Nothing lying in the road. Nothing lying in the scrub brush on the side of the road. I got back in the car and was about to drive away when a large man in rags rushed out of the woods at us. His arms were outstretched, his fingers were gnarled and curled, his hair was patchy and clogged with dirt. His skin was dark and shredding off his face. His eyes were glowing red.

"YOW!" Lula yelled. "In the name of the father and the son and the holy someone else . . ."

The raggedy creature slammed himself against the car, grabbing for the door handle.

"I can smell him!" Lula shrieked. "Carnations and doodie! It's hideous. I'm going to throw up. I'm going to poop."

I stomped on the gas, and the Lexus jumped forward. The raggedy thing lost its grip, and I sped away.

I turned onto Broad with my hands clenched on the steering wheel and my heart pounding in my chest. Breathe, I told myself. Relax the fingers. Concentrate on the road.

I cut my eyes to Lula. "You didn't, did you?"

"What?"

"Poop yourself."

"I don't think so. I'm almost positive. But I need a drink, or a donut, or bacon. I don't even have a word for what happened back there."

I didn't have a word for it either. I hit something I couldn't identify. I heard some scary sounds coming from the woods. Something charged my car. It looked like a zombie. Don't even go there, I thought. Zombies only live in Hollywood. Okay, and

I feel stupid thinking that it might have been a zombie, but I saw it, and it looked like a zombie. Truth is, I saw something else. I saw a teenage boy standing in the middle of the road. I saw it for a split second before the big raggedy man rushed out of the woods at me. When I turned my attention back to the road the boy was gone.

"Did you see a boy in the middle of the road?" I asked Lula.

"A boy? Like a zombie boy?"

"No. An ordinary boy. Maybe fourteen or fifteen."

"I didn't see nothing but my life flashing in front of me. I'll tell you what would be a good idea. They should stuff the chicken's head up its butt with the rest of the giblets. Then it would be there if you need it."

FOURTEEN

I VERY CAREFULLY and deliberately drove to the office. I parked at the curb, and Lula and I got out and looked at the Lexus. It had a dent and a gash in the front right quarter panel, and a strip of filthy cloth was caught in the gash.

"That's a zombie rag," Lula said. "I'd know it anywhere. It even smells like zombie. Boy, I'm glad I'm not the one who ran over him. They got no sense of humor about stuff like that. Zombies are mean buggers. You piss them off and they come to get you."

"How do you know so much about zombies?"

"I saw that Brad Pitt movie. And then I googled zombies."

Connie came out of the office and looked at the Lexus.

"What happened?" she asked.

"Stephanie ran over a zombie," Lula said.

Connie looked at me. "Really?"

"I ran over *something*. I guess it looked like a zombie."

"Bummer," Connie said.

"Yeah, it's a problem on account of you don't want to piss off a zombie," Lula said. "Am I right?"

I pulled the rag off the car and tossed it into the back seat with the rotisserie chicken. "See you tomorrow."

"Hope so," Lula said. "Remember, in case they come to get you, you have to shoot them in the brain, so you should put some bullets in your gun."

I gave Lula a thumbs-up, and I got back into the Lexus. Lula was right about the rag. It didn't smell good. When you combined it with the chicken it was a total gag. I called Morelli and asked where he was.

"Home," he said. "And I can actually spend the night here unless someone finds a headless body."

"I'm on my way," I said. "I have something to show you."

"I have something to show you too."

"We might not be on the same page."

"Work with me," Morelli said.

Ten minutes later, I walked into Morelli's house, and Bob galloped in from the kitchen to greet me. He got to the middle of the living room and stopped. His nose twitched, hackles rose on his back, and he growled. The only other time I've heard him growl was when he stole a Virginia baked ham off the table and Morelli tried to get it back.

Morelli came up behind Bob.

"What's going on?" he asked. "What's that smell? Did you run over another outhouse?"

"I ran over a zombie." I held the rag out for him to see. "This is what's left of him."

"What's in the other bag?"

"Rotisserie chicken."

Morelli grinned. "That's a killer combination."

"I thought you might want someone to examine the cloth."

"And the chicken?"

"Dinner."

"I like it," Morelli said. "I'll put the zombie attack dog in the backyard."

I followed him into the kitchen and put the piece of cloth into a plastic baggie while he carved the chicken.

"Tell me about the cloth," he said.

I washed my hands and set the kitchen table with plates and silverware, and Morelli brought the chicken to the table.

"I took some chicken to Ethel this afternoon, and when I stepped out of the double-wide I heard creepy growly moaning sounds coming from the woods. I looked into the woods, and I saw two sets of glowing red eyes that were attached to two bodies that looked human. The bodies were in shadow, and I couldn't see any details, but it freaked me out enough to want to get out of there."

"You were alone?"

"Lula was with me. We jumped into my car and took off. I was a short distance down Diggery's road when this *thing* jumped out in front of me, and I bounced him off my right front quarter panel. I stopped and got out of the car, but the *thing* was gone. Lula was sure it was a zombie."

"Did you think it was a zombie?" Morelli asked.

"It happened so fast that I barely saw it. Honestly, it could have been a velociraptor or a unicorn. Anyway, I got back into the car, and I was about to drive away when this man, for lack of a better word, came out of the woods and rushed the car. I'm no expert but it looked a lot like a zombie. Dirt-clogged hair, rotting skin, raggedy clothes. It grabbed the door handle, but I had the car locked."

"And?"

"And I drove away. Fast. When I got to the office I looked at the car. There's a dent and a gash in the right front quarter panel, and the cloth was caught in the ripped part."

"And you think it was a zombie?"

"I think it *looked* like a zombie. And Lula said it smelled like a zombie."

Morelli wiped his hands on a paper towel. "Let's look at your car."

We went outside, and Morelli walked around the Lexus.

"Ranger?" he asked.

"Yep."

Ranger wasn't Morelli's favorite person for many reasons, not the least of which is my ongoing relationship with the man.

"Nice car," Morelli said.

I nodded. "Except it has a dent in it."

Morelli was on one knee, examining the dent and the torn fiberglass. "I don't see any blood, but I'd like to have CSI go over this."

"Sure."

"And I'll give them the cloth."

"Do you think it was a zombie?"

"No," Morelli said. "I also don't think it was a velociraptor or a unicorn."

"I need dessert. Do you have any ice cream?"

"Yes. Chocolate. Do you know what I need?"

"Yep," I said. "I have a pretty good idea. Can I have my ice cream first?"

"As long as you eat fast."

FIFTEEN

MORELLI SHOOK ME awake at six o'clock. The room was dark, and I wasn't ready to start my day. It had been a long, satisfying, but exhausting night.

"I'm heading out," he said. "I'm going to trade cars with you so CSI can take a look at yours."

"They're just going to look at the quarter panel, right?"

There was a beat of silence. "Something you want to tell me about the car?" he asked.

"It's a Rangeman car. It's . . . equipped."

"Legally equipped?"

I brushed hair back from my face. "I don't even know what that means."

"I'll check the car out before I turn it over," Morelli said. "I'm not going to get blown up, am I?"

"Maybe you should call Ranger first."

Morelli grunted. "My favorite thing to do."

"I thought you did your favorite thing last night. And then you did your second favorite and third favorite."

He smiled, his teeth white in the dark room. "You wouldn't let me do my fourth favorite."

"You can permanently wipe that off the list. That's disgusting."

He kissed me on my forehead and left.

• • •

It was almost nine o'clock when I rolled into the office. I'd made a stop at my apartment to shower and change clothes. Diesel wasn't there, and the bed hadn't been slept in. I had a twinge of anxiety over his safety and gave myself a mental slap in the face. He was fine. He was always fine. In fact, he might be immortal.

Connie was applying clear coat to her nails when I walked in, and Lula was pacing.

"I got a case of nerves," Lula said. "I'm worried about the zombies. This could be the start of something. There could be an apocalypse coming. And what about the ones that are already walking around? How long before they stop looking for dead brains and start going after live brains? It could be any day now. And our brains are going to be at the top of their list because you ran over one of them and ripped off some of his rags."

Lula's hair was au naturel today, resulting in a massive, impenetrable afro. I thought the zombies would have a hard time getting to Lula's brain.

"How about you?" Lula asked me. "Aren't you nervous? Weren't you agitated over the zombies all last night?"

I shook my head. "I spent the night with Morelli. I was agitated over other things."

"Did you tell him you punted a zombie?"

"Yes. I gave him the piece of cloth. He's going to have it tested today. And he swapped cars with me so the lab guys could take a look at that too."

"You've got one sexy guy who gives you cars, and another sexy guy who agitates you," Lula said. "It's not fair that you have two sexy guys, and I'm depending on battery-operated devices."

It got better or worse depending on your point of view. There was a third guy in my life. I wasn't sure what role he played, but he was definitely sexy.

"We have two open files," I said. "Chucci and Slick. I'm curious about Slick. I say we check on him first."

"I guess that would be okay," Lula said, "but if I smell carnations and outhouse I'm out of there."

"Fair enough."

We left the office, and Lula was relieved to see we'd be using Morelli's green SUV.

"This is good," she said. "This is an unrecognizable car for the zombies. They won't immediately know who we are when we park in the cemetery lot."

I buckled up and pulled away from the curb. "You need to stop obsessing about zombies. They aren't real. Something bad is happening, but it's not the result of a zombie uprising."

"How can you be sure?"

I didn't have an answer for this. It was like believing in God. You did or you didn't. Or in my case, I wasn't sure so I hedged my bets by going to mass at Christmas. And I only used the Lord's name in vain under extreme circumstances.

"I just don't think there are zombies," I said.

"So what did we see?"

"I don't know. Something made up to look like a zombie."

"What about the glowing red eyes?"

"I have to admit, they were freaky."

"Fuckin' A," Lula said.

I parked in the cemetery lot, and Lula and I walked to the gate. Lula had her gun drawn in case she had to shoot a zombie in the brain. My gun was at home in the cookie jar. The Rangeman gun was riding along with Morelli. I kept telling myself I didn't believe in zombies, and mostly I didn't. I also didn't believe in giant spiders that could eat me alive and venom-spewing, anal-probing aliens from Uranus. All this not believing had little effect on the irrational fear I carried for zombies, spiders, and aliens.

We passed through the gate, and Lula stopped and sniffed.

"Well?" I asked.

"It smells okay. And I'm not getting any zombie vibes. I say we keep going."

We followed the path to the tree where Slick had set up camp. The area was littered with his belongings, but he wasn't there. A white Styrofoam cooler was overturned and empty. A blanket, his GoPro, his journal, and a ball cap were on the ground by the cooler.

"I don't like the looks of this," Lula said.

"Maybe he had to use the bathroom."

"Or maybe the zombies got him."

It bothered me that Slick's GoPro and journal were lying out, and that the pen was several feet from the journal. I was trying not to be an alarmist, but I secretly agreed with Lula that this didn't look good.

Lula was standing by a tombstone, staring at the grave. "Does it look like someone started to dig this up again?"

"Yes. Some of the sod has been dislodged."

I walked farther down the path, finding another grave that had been recently disturbed. Lula's video camera was half buried in the soft dirt. I shouted for Slick, but no one answered. The cemetery was eerily quiet.

I called Morelli, gave him the short version, and suggested he might want to take a look at the grave sites.

Lula returned to the parking lot to direct the police when they arrived, and I stayed graveside. I knew there was a good chance that this was a crime scene and I needed to keep its integrity, but I wanted to read Slick's journal and see what he'd caught on the cameras.

I carefully brushed the dirt away from Lula's camera and checked recent videos. There was nothing after Lula's bungee-jumping disaster. I placed the camera back in the dirt and went to the GoPro. The rewind on this showed more. Two shadowy forms with glowing eyes could be seen moving toward the camera.

Slick's voice was a whisper. "Oh, no. Oh crap."

The creatures stopped and looked left. Slick panned with the camera, and I saw a third form. It was taller, and it quickly moved out of the frame. The camera was on infrared mode, making identification difficult, but there was something about the hair and the build of the third one that looked familiar. I replayed the video and had a chilling feeling in my gut. I couldn't be certain, but I thought it looked like Diesel. The camera returned to the two red-eyed creatures as they rushed at Slick, arms outstretched, mouths gaping open. The video went to the dark sky, someone screamed, and the camera cut out.

I heard cars entering the parking lot, and I was in a state of confused anxiety. I was having a hard time breathing and thinking. The red-eyed creatures in the video were terrifying. Slick was missing, and my stomach was sick at the possibility of finding his headless body behind a tombstone. And then there was Diesel. I was almost positive he was the man in the video. What the heck was he doing there? Was he one of them? Was he hunting them? And what was I supposed to say to Morelli? *I think I recognize the tall guy in the video. He's living with me. And he's been sleeping in my bed. Naked.* This brought on more nausea.

Okay, get a grip. Breathe. It's not so bad. It's all been pretty innocent. No penetration. No exchange of bodily fluids. Not yet, anyway. And now that he might be a zombie, or maybe a zombie handler . . . I squinched my eyes closed. Don't even go there. First off, there are no zombies. Second, there are no zombies.

Two uniforms appeared on the path, and I realized I hadn't

looked at the journal. I dropped the GoPro, snatched the journal off the ground, and shoved it into my bag. I made the sign of the cross and told God I was only keeping the journal for a short time. It wasn't like I was stealing something or tampering with evidence. I was actually *safeguarding* evidence so it didn't get trampled by all the cops who were rushing into the cemetery.

Morelli was close behind the uniforms. I stood to one side and waited for him to first take in the scene at the grave and then make his way to me.

"Let me get this straight," Morelli said. "Instead of taking Slick in, you decided to let him stay here to film the zombies."

"At the time, it sounded like an okay idea."

Morelli looked at the GoPro lying on the ground. "He was going to film them with this?"

"Yes. And with a camera that Lula loaned him. We found Lula's camera at the other grave."

"And no one's touched any of this?"

"Pretty much."

Small grimace from Morelli. "And?"

"There's nothing on Lula's camera, but the GoPro shows a couple guys with glowing red eyes coming at Slick."

Morelli pulled on gloves, picked the camera up, and watched the rewind.

"What do you think?" I asked him.

"Zombies," Morelli said. "No doubt about it."

He watched it a second time. "There's someone on this video who doesn't look like a zombie."

"Hmmm," I said. "I must have missed that."

"He's at a distance, and he's only on camera for a heartbeat. I'll have the tech enhance the frame, and I'll take another look."

"How about the zombies? Did you recognize either of them?"

"I thought one looked a little like Bugs Molinowski, but Bugs isn't dead yet."

"Would that matter?"

"Tape this off," Morelli said to one of the uniforms. "And get it photographed."

"Do you want to see the other disturbed grave?" I asked him.

"Sure. Disturbed graves are my favorite. Right behind headless bodies."

I led him along the path to the second grave, and Morelli knelt down and scooped up some earth.

"The tombstone says this woman was buried seven months ago," Morelli said, "but this is a fresh dig, and there was no attempt made to hide it. A professional like Diggery would have replaced the sod."

"He takes pride in his work," I said.

Morelli stood and looked around. "And he doesn't want to get caught. Have you gone through the rest of the cemetery?"

"No. I called you when I saw this, and I went back to Slick's sleepover spot."

"I'll have it canvassed, and I'll let you know if we find Slick."

"Likewise," I said.

He cut his eyes to the path to make sure we were alone. He wrapped an arm around me and kissed me.

"Last night was good," he said. "With any luck, I won't be working tonight either."

"That would be great. I love when we get to spend the night together. Especially at your house. It's so comfy."

I wasn't sure I'd survive a second night in a row with Morelli, but I was going to give it my all, because I absolutely wasn't going to share a bed with Diesel. In fact, I might even move Rex temporarily to my mother's house. I had no clue what Diesel's relationship was to the zombie people, but I didn't want to take a chance on someone drilling a hole in Rex's head and sucking out his tiny hamster brain for an hors d'oeuvre.

"When will I get my car back?" I asked.

"They're going over the car now. I'll bring it home with me."

SIXTEEN

LULA WAS WAITING in the cemetery parking lot.

"What's going on in there?" she asked.

"Not much. They're doing their cop thing."

"Any sign of Slick?"

"No, but the police are just starting to look."

"What about us?"

"We're going to look for Johnny Chucci."

"I think his brother was telling us a fib, and Johnny's with him. Johnny was driving his car. And I'd talk to the ex-wife. I bet he's creeping around her house, looking in her windows. We should go there at night. That's when obsessed lunatics go creeping. Only thing is I don't know if I want to go out at night, what with the zombies roaming everywhere. Have you noticed they're all over Trenton? I'd think they'd stay close to their cemetery. I mean, how did they get to the hardware store? Do they drive? Do they have zombie cars? Do they cart their decapitated heads around in cabs or Uber cars?"

I hadn't thought about it. It was a good question.

Ranger called on my cellphone. "Babe, your car is at the police station, but your messenger bag is at the cemetery on Morley Street."

"I kind of punted a zombie off the right front quarter panel yesterday. The police are looking at the car for DNA and stuff."

There was silence on Ranger's end, and I thought I caught a single burst of muffled laughter.

"Are you laughing?" I asked him.

"Yes. What happened to the zombie?"

"He disappeared."

"Hard to take down a zombie," Ranger said. "Was the car totaled?"

"No. I'm still working on that."

"Counting down the days," Ranger said.

. . .

I drove past Little Pinkie's gym on my way to the Burg.

"I don't see a silver Honda in the lot," Lula said. "Are we going to stop in again?"

"No. Johnny isn't going to be at the gym, and Little Pinkie isn't going to help me find him. I'm going to take another look at Little Pinkie's house, and then I'm going to talk to the ex-wife."

"I like that plan. I'm interested in the ex-wife. What would possess a woman to take up painting gnomes? It's sick, but in a good way, you see what I'm saying? I think she must be a unique individual."

It was almost eleven o'clock by the time I cruised past Little Pinkie's house. A driveway led to a detached single-car garage that sat at the back of the property. There were no cars in front of the house and no cars in the driveway. I circled the block and parked one house down from Little Pinkie on the same side of the road.

Lula and I went to the door and rang the bell. No one answered, but the dog repeated his barking, snarling routine. Lula walked around and looked in the first-floor windows. I walked back to the garage and looked in the single grimy side-door window. We met back at the front of the house.

"Well?" Lula asked.

"The garage is empty. No car."

"And I didn't see any people. I guess someone could be upstairs, but there was nothing that said a freeloading guest was hanging out."

I cut across the Burg to the ex-wife's, and we picked our way through the gnomes to the front door.

"The advantage to this is you don't have to cut the grass, being that there isn't any," Lula said. "This lady got wall-to-wall gnomes."

I rang the bell, and Judy Chucci opened the door. She was a couple inches shorter than me and pleasantly plump. That's an outdated expression, but it fit Judy Chucci perfectly. She had brown hair tucked back behind her ears, and she was wearing jeans and a gray sweatshirt. The sweatshirt looked like someone had dripped red paint on it or maybe had a massive nosebleed.

"Omigod," she said. "Stephanie Plum, right? You used to hang out with my little sister, Joanie. Joanie Beam."

"Wow," I said. "I didn't know you were Joanie's sister."

"Yeah, I get that a lot. We don't look alike, right? She's all blond and thin, and I'm, you know, round."

"What's she doing now? I haven't seen her in years."

"She works at the tattoo parlor on State Street, downtown. She's real good. I saw her tattoo Madonna on a guy once."

"It's gotta be hard to do Madonna," Lula said. "I guess being artistic runs in the family. Looks like your thing is gnomes."

"A lot of people don't understand the finer points of gnome painting," Judy said. "At first glance, they might all look the same, but it's the details that count. Charlie, over in the corner, has a little pink in his red coat. And Harry, by the mailbox, has a crooked smile. And poor Mr. Murphy has a cataract. It was an accident. I added too much white to his eyes and next thing he was blind." Judy bit into her lower lip. "I'm so sorry," she whispered to Mr. Murphy.

"Can't you just paint over it?" Lula asked.

Judy shook her head. "No. He's blind. It's irreversible."

"That's too bad," Lula said. "Seems like something could be done to help him."

"I'm told there's a paint specialist in Denver who does wonderful work," Judy said. "I've started a GoFundMe page for Mr. Murphy."

"That's a excellent idea," Lula said. "I hear those pages rake in big bucks. And they got a good variety of weed in Denver, too."

Judy nodded. "Mr. Murphy would like that. And he deserves it. He's suffered so much."

"About Johnny," I said.

Judy stiffened and looked around. "He better not be here. I have a restraining order."

"He missed his court date," I said. "I work for his bond agent, and I need to bring him in to get rescheduled. I was hoping you'd help me find him."

"In other words, you want to take him to jail?"

"Yes."

"I'm in. What do you want to know? What do I have to do?"

"Boy, you must really dislike him," Lula said.

"He's a douchebag," Judy said, "but I don't want to get into that in front of the gnomes." Judy stepped back. "Would you like to come in? I have coffee cake."

We followed Judy along a narrow path through the living room. There were gnomes on every surface. They were on the floor, on the tables, on the couch, and on all the chairs. Ditto the dining room and kitchen. She had a gnome-painting workstation set up on the kitchen table.

"You ever watch that television show about hoarders?" Lula asked Judy.

"Yeah, those poor people get buried alive with their stuff. I don't know why they don't get help."

"You ever see any hoarder shows about gnomes?"

Judy was searching through her kitchen. "I know I have a coffee cake here somewhere."

"That's okay," I said. "We don't really have time for coffee cake. I was hoping you could give me some information on Johnny. Do you know where he's staying?"

"From what I hear, he moves around. Nobody can tolerate him for more than two days. He's *so annoying*. He has an opinion about everything. Talk, talk, talk. And he's constantly cracking his knuckles, and there's no polite way to say this . . . he farts. A lot."

"Maybe he's got gluten issues," Lula said.

"Maybe he should double up on his underwear in the place that counts, instead of wearing a pair on his head," Judy said.

"Does he have a favorite bar or fast-food place?" I asked. "Is there any place he regularly hangs out?"

"Yes," Judy said. "Here! I have a restraining order against him because he skulks around my house every night and breaks my gnomes, but that doesn't stop him. He leaves stupid presents on my doorstep."

"What kind of presents?" Lula asked.

"Flowers and bottles of wine and pizza and jewelry."

"They sound like nice presents," Lula said.

"I guess so, but he's such an oaf he's always knocking over the gnomes. He broke Henry's arm last night. I call the police and by the time they get here he's gone."

"Where does he get the money to buy these presents?" I asked. "Does he have a job?"

"He steals them," Judy said. "The moron puts his underpants on his head and steals stuff."

"Does he have a routine?" I asked. "When does he leave these presents?"

"Usually between nine and eleven. He knows I go to bed at eleven."

"I'm going to stake out your house between nine and eleven for a couple days," I said. "Don't call the police. Maybe I can catch Johnny."

Lula and I tiptoed our way through the gnomes to Morelli's car.

"If you ask me, they're both whackadoodle," Lula said, buckling her seatbelt.

I was about to drive to the office when my mother called.

"You have to come see this," she said. "You have to talk to your grandmother. And I've got kielbasa for lunch."

"We're having lunch at my parents' house," I said to Lula.

• • •

Grandma met us at the door. Her hair was cut, styled, and colored to look exactly like my mom's. And Grandma was spray-tanned. Head to toe with the exception of white circles around her eyes.

"What do you think?" she asked.

"I think you rock," Lula said. "Us girls gotta mix it up once in a while."

"I'm taking it for a test-drive," Grandma said.

My mom was in the kitchen.

"I heard that," she said. "As long as you don't test-drive it to Florida."

I led the way and hung my bag on a kitchen chair. The small table was set for four, and the bread and butter were already out.

"Hey, Mrs. P.," Lula said. "It smells good in here."

"Kielbasa and sauerkraut," my mom said. "It's lunch, so everyone helps themselves from the pot on the stove."

We all filled our plates and sat at the table.

"Look at her," my mother said, cutting her eyes to Grandma. "She's going to Florida. I'm going to come back from mass someday and she'll be gone. And who knows about this man. He could be a serial killer, a white slaver. He could be one of those men who steals Social Security from old women."

"He has a good job working in a bar," Grandma said. "He's a family man. He can't help if he looks hot. And my Social Security isn't worth crap. I wouldn't be living here if I got any kind of money from Social Security."

"I want you to do a background check on him," my mom said to me. "I know you have all those programs that you use to track down criminals. I want you to find out about this *person*."

"That's reasonable," Lula said. "I always check up on the men I go out with. There's some freaks out there."

"I guess that's okay," Grandma said. "I'm sure he has nothing to hide."

I took down all the information on Roger Murf, and promised I'd get right to it. Truth is, I agreed with my mom and Lula. It was a good idea. Hard to have a lot of trust in a guy who looks like George Hamilton.

Lula and I laid waste to the kielbasa, insincerely offered to help with cleanup, and left.

"I'm somewhat of an expert on sausage," Lula said when we

were in the car, "and that was about the best sausage ever. I wouldn't mind knowing how to cook a sausage like that, but probably I'd need a stove."

Lula had half a fridge, a Keurig, and a single-induction burner. At least she had an excuse for not cooking. I had zip.

I drove past all the real estate associated with Johnny Chucci and didn't see the silver Honda. I called Morelli and asked about Slick. He said they'd searched the entire cemetery and its surroundings and didn't find Slick or any of his body parts.

"I'm at a temporary dead end," I said to Lula. "I'm going to drop you at the office and head home to research Grandma's boyfriend. Do you want to stake out the gnome house with me tonight?"

"Wouldn't miss it. With any luck, Chucci will show up, and he'll still have his underpants on his head."

SEVENTEEN

I LET MYSELF into my apartment and paused. No television sounds. No men's shoes kicked off in the living room. No one singing in the shower.

"Hello?" I called.

Silence.

I hung my bag on a hook in the foyer and walked through the apartment. No Diesel. Good deal. I was happy to delay the confrontation. I sat at the dining room table, opened my laptop, and ran Roger Murf through a couple search programs. Nothing derogatory turned up. He had good credit. His work history checked out. He had two adult children living in New Jersey. And he had a wife in Key West. Whoops.

I ran the wife, Miriam Murf, through the search programs, and she showed the same residence and credit history as Roger. Files indicated that they'd been married for forty years, and that she was still alive.

I couldn't find any photos, so I called Connie. She has more advanced search programs than I do, and she has Florida connections. I fed her my information, and she said she'd get back to me. I suppose I didn't really need a photo, but I wanted to see if he actually looked like George Hamilton.

• • •

Morelli called at four o'clock.

"What's new?" I asked.

"Are you sure you want to know?"

"Is it bad?"

"I got the autopsy report back on the homeless victim."

"The one with the hole in his head?"

"Yeah. He had blunt force trauma to the back of his head. It appears that he was knocked unconscious, and then had his brain removed. This is the first victim who seems to have been killed by the brain snatcher. All others were already deceased."

"I don't get it. How do the zombies remove the brain?"

"Big straw?"

"That's not funny."

"I was being serious."

Ugh!

"What about Slick?" I asked.

"No sign of him. I'm on my way to talk to his parents."

"Would you like me to pick something up for dinner and bring it to your house?"

"That would be great. Bring something that can be reheated in case I'm late."

"How late?"

There was a beat of silence. "Does it matter?" Morelli asked.

"I'm staking out Judy Chucci's house tonight from nine to eleven."

"I'm pretty sure I'll be home by eleven."

"If you come home later than that I'll be the woman in your bed."

"I like it."

I disconnected, went to the foyer, and pulled Slick's notebook out of my messenger bag. I returned to the table and started reading. I drifted into a coma on page five. Oprah might love it. Me not so much. It was about a person named Zero who was a lost soul. Zero had given up his humanoid and sexual identity and was wandering naked in the woods. The idea was interesting but the writing was atrocious. Zero explained on page one that he was inventing a new writing form called stream of unconsciousness, and that he didn't believe in the use of punctuation.

I skimmed from page five on. Not a lot happened to Zero. Mostly Zero was thinking about food and having sex with itself. These were complicated issues for Zero because, having no identity, he didn't know what he was supposed to eat. The sex came easier, and was explained in great detail, but was difficult to follow without punctuation. On page twenty-two, Zero wrote about coming across another *thing*. It didn't have a name, but it was also having sex with itself. Fortunately, the writing ended on page twenty-three, shortly after ejaculation. Hard to tell which of them was ejaculating. Maybe both.

• • •

I got baked beans and pulled pork from the deli and fresh-made rolls from the bakery. Morelli wasn't home when I arrived at his house, so I stowed the beans and the pork in the fridge, and I put the rolls in the cupboard where Bob couldn't get at them. Bob and I went for a walk around a bunch of blocks, and when we returned to the house, it was still empty. I fed Bob and made myself a pulled pork sandwich. I called Morelli, but he didn't pick up.

It was eight-thirty when I fetched Lula.

"Did you notice how I'm all dressed in black for night surveillance?" Lula said, buckling herself in. "Between my black clothes and my chocolate skin, I'm a total shadow. I'm like invisible. I'm the black bomb."

I was dressed in the same clothes I'd worn all day, and my skin did me no favors when it came to the shadow-blending thing. Fortunately, I was average enough that I almost never attracted attention.

I parked Morelli's car on the opposite side of the street from Judy Chucci's house, and Lula and I settled in to wait. Lights were on in her house but curtains were drawn. It was an overcast night. No moon. By nine o'clock I realized I was going to have to leave the car and get closer to the house. It would be too easy for Johnny to sneak around in the dark, drop a package on Judy's porch, and run off into the night.

Lula and I crossed the street and hid behind a car belonging to the neighbor next door. There was no street traffic. Residents were inside watching television, putting kids to bed, and Facebooking.

"I can't wait to see what present Judy's getting tonight," Lula said. "It's like she got Christmas every day."

I checked my watch at nine-thirty. "Not a creature is stirring, not even a mouse," I said to Lula.

"Tell me about it," Lula said. "This is tedious. I'm tired of standing here. I can't even do anything on my phone on account of the screen would light up."

"I think I just saw movement on the far side of Judy's house," I whispered.

We froze and squinted into the darkness.

"I see it," Lula said. "It's him. I can see his raggedy undies on his head."

I didn't see any undies. I saw a shadowy figure move in front of a tree and disappear. I thought I heard the rustle of cloth, or maybe it was something brushing against the tree.

"Wait until he goes to the door," I whispered. "We don't want to have to chase him through everyone's backyard in the dark."

"Sure, I get that," Lula said, "but what if he doesn't go to her front door? What if he's going to her back door? I'm gonna sneak between these two houses, and see if he's at the back door."

"No!"

Too late. She was off and tippy-toe running to the back of the house. And then she was out of sight, around the corner of the building.

"Stop!" she shouted. "You're under arrest, sort of. Actually, we can't arrest you, but we can apprehend you."

I took off at a dead run. It was pitch-black between the houses, and there wasn't much light at the back. I heard something crash. I heard Lula cussing. More crashing.

"Damn fucking gnomes," Lula said.

I turned into the backyard and ran into a gnome.

"I got him!" Lula yelled. "I got Mr. Underpants! I got... *YOW!*"

She was on the other side of the yard, by the back door, and there were about a hundred gnomes between us.

"Help!" Lula yelled. "Holy crap!"

I kicked a bunch of gnomes out of the way and crossed the yard. I saw Lula but no Johnny.

"Did he get away?" I asked.

Lula was dancing around. "It was a zombie. I touched a zombie. I got zombie cooties. It was awful. He smelled like doodie and carnations. I can't get it out of my nose. I gotta cut off my nose. Get me a knife."

"Are you sure it was a zombie?"

"I got cooties. I got cooties. They're on my clothes. He grabbed me, and he touched my clothes."

Lula ripped her black spandex tank top off and peeled her black spandex tights off. She was left wearing a black thong.

"Good God," I said. "If you take any more off you're not getting in Morelli's car."

"It's the cooties. I can feel them on me. They're zombie cooties. They're the worst kind."

"Are you sure they aren't Johnny Chucci cooties?"

"He had bad breath, too. His breath smelled like dirt and worms."

"He breathed on you?"

"It was awful."

The back-porch light flashed on, and Judy stepped out. "What's happening? Did you catch Johnny?"

"You got any bleach?" Lula asked. "I gotta pour bleach on myself."

Judy looked at the backyard. "My gnomes! What happened to my gnomes? Where's Mr. Sunshine Sparkle?"

"We just got here," I said. "It looks like someone tried to run through your yard."

"Yeah," Lula said. "It might have been a pack of wild dogs. Or maybe the zombies."

Judy blinked. "Zombies?"

"They're all over town," Lula said. "Trenton's lousy with them. They were probably here looking for gnome brains."

"That's horrible," Judy said.

"No shit," Lula said. "You might want to take your gnomes in the house . . . what's left of them anyways."

"You haven't got any clothes on," Judy said to Lula.

"My clothes got the cooties," Lula said.

Judy grimaced, stepped into her house, and closed and locked the door.

"I should have shot him in the head," Lula said. "It's that he caught me by surprise."

"Next time," I told her.

"Yeah, I'll be ready next time."

I looked at her clothes lying on the ground. "What are you going to do about your clothes?"

"I'm not touching them. They can rot there. They been tarnished with zombie juju."

"You're only wearing a thong."

"And?"

"I'm feeling uncomfortable."

"Maybe because you've never been a 'ho. You get used to this when you're a 'ho. You get comfortable with naked shit."

"So, you're going home like that?"

"Is it a problem?"

I blew out a sigh. "No, but if we get stopped by the police you have to hold me at gunpoint and say you forced me to drive you like this."

"Sure. I could do that."

I drove Lula across town without incident, and dropped her at her house. I waited until she was safe inside, and then I drove to my apartment. I idled in the lot and looked up at my windows. No lights were on. No flicker from a television screen. Probably no Diesel. I parked, walked into the building, and took the stairs to my apartment. We have an elevator, but it's unreliable and frequently smells like take-out burrito.

I flipped the kitchen light on and said hello to Rex. I gave him fresh water, filled his cup with hamster food, and gave him a Ritz cracker. I shoved some clean clothes into a tote bag, and debated giving Morelli the notebook I'd lifted from the cemetery. In the end, I decided against it. There was nothing to be gained from the journal, and it would only complicate things.

Diesel's leather knapsack was still stashed in a corner, so I assumed he'd be back. It didn't look to me like the bed had been slept in since I departed it, and there were no dirty dishes in the kitchen. I had a squishy feeling in my stomach that something bad might have happened to Diesel. I hoped this wasn't the case. I hoped he wasn't a zombie. And I hoped he wasn't married.

I ignored the squishy stomach, said good night to Rex, and left my apartment.

. . .

I parked in front of Morelli's house, and he pulled in behind me in Ranger's Lexus NX. He wrapped an arm around me, hugged me close, and kissed me.

"I'm beat," he said. "And I'm starving, but I think if I could get something to eat I could muster enough energy to get you naked."

"I brought pulled pork."

"That'll do it," Morelli said.

We sat at the little kitchen table, and Morelli dug in.

"I'm guessing you still haven't found Slick," I said.

"No. No head. No brain. No body. I talked to his parents, but they weren't helpful. I'm waiting for the tech to isolate the zombie frames for me."

"Did anything interesting turn up at the cemetery?"

"We exhumed the second grave, and everything seemed to be untouched."

"And the first one?"

"Empty."

"Excuse me?"

"Not for common knowledge, but it was empty. No casket. Nothing but dirt."

"Do you think Diggery took it on one of his earlier digs?"

"Diggery doesn't usually do that. He robs everything on the scene and covers his tracks."

"Maybe the zombies got rid of the casket, so it was easier to escape through their portal."

"That would be one theory."

"Do you have any others?"

"No." He made himself a second sandwich. "How was your night? Did you catch Johnny?"

"Lula had a run-in with a zombie in Judy Chucci's backyard. The zombie got away, but Lula was convinced she was contaminated with zombie cooties, and she stripped down to her thong."

"Whoa! That had to be frightening."

"The zombie?"

"Yeah, that too."

"I didn't see the zombie."

"How did Lula know it was a zombie?"

"It sounded like they were up close and personal. She said it breathed on her."

"Okay. That's close. Did she get any pieces of zombie rag? Was there an exchange of zombie fluid?"

"It wasn't *that* personal."

Morelli got a beer out of the fridge. "Worth asking."

"What about *my* zombie rag?"

"I haven't got the report back yet. Not sure what they got off the car other than a look at state-of-the-art tracking technology and a legal Glock that refused to hold a fingerprint. Unfortunately, it's a Friday so I might not know anything until Monday."

"Are you working tomorrow?"

"I'm on call. Are you working?"

"The office is open for a half day. I need to check on Ethel, and Connie is doing some research for me."

EIGHTEEN

LULA AND CONNIE were already at the office when I walked in. Connie was dressed down in jeans and sneakers and a red sweater. Lula was wearing chunky gladiator sandals, a short black metallic skirt, and a silver tank top. If I didn't know her I might have been frightened. She looked like a *Who's Your Mama?* dominatrix.

"I have your photos," Connie said. "Roger and Miriam Murf."

Lula came over to see the photos. "Who we looking at?"

"Grandma's boyfriend and his wife," I said.

"Say what?"

The only thing Roger Murf had in common with George Hamilton was a tan. Murf was short, mostly bald, and overweight. His wife was equally tan, equally overweight, and excessively wrinkled. Their photos came from the DMV and from an article about a senior center swingers club.

"They need a good dermatologist," Lula said.

I took the photos from Connie and stuffed them into my messenger bag.

"I'll run these over to Grandma, and then I'm going to check on Ethel."

Lula looked out the office front window. "You got the zombie car back. I don't know if it's a good idea for you to go down Diggery's road with that car. There could be zombies lurking that remember you drove over one of them."

"We could take your car."

"No way. Even if we didn't hit any zombies it would get all dusty."

I tried not to roll my eyes, but I was only partially successful. "Okay, I'll drive. Are you coming?"

"Hell, yeah. Somebody's got to be there to shoot the zombies."

• • •

I left Lula in the car, and I ran to my parents' house. Grandma was in the foyer, holding her purse.

"Are you going somewhere?" I asked.

"I got a date."

"You aren't going to Florida, are you?"

"No. That's old business," Grandma said. "I'm moving on. I don't know if I want to keep up with a man who looks like George Hamilton. You got to put a lot of work into looking that good. Besides I got a new honey. This tan and hairdo got me a date with Willie Kuber. He used to be a butcher at Giovichinni's. We're going to the shore to play skillo."

"Wow. That's great."

"I'm pretty stoked," Grandma said. "He could be the one. I've had my eye on him ever since his wife passed. For an older man, he's got a real nice bum."

I told Grandma to have fun, and I hurried back to Lula.

"Did you break the news to her?" Lula asked.

"Wasn't necessary. She has a date with Willie Kuber. They're going to the shore to play skillo."

"I don't know who that is, but playing skillo is an excellent date idea."

I drove out of the Burg and took Broad Street to Diggery's neighborhood. Halfway to his double-wide I almost ran over a groundhog. It was sneakers-up in the middle of the single-lane road.

I stopped, and Lula and I peered over the hood at the brown blob.

"Looks like a big ol' groundhog," Lula said.

"Yeah, a big ol' *dead* groundhog. I can't drive around it, but I think I'll clear if I drive over it."

"Yeah, but what if it *isn't* dead, and you don't clear it? Then you got more blood on your hands. First you mow down a zombie, and now you risk smooshing a groundhog. Maybe this groundhog's just taking a nap."

I blew my horn at the groundhog. Nothing.

"He could be deaf," Lula said.

"I think you should get out of the car, and poke it with a stick, and take a real close look at it," I said.

"I'll get out, if you'll get out."

"Great. Fine. I'll get out. *Yeesh*."

I wrenched the door open, lurched out, and went to stand over the slightly bloated groundhog. Lula came up beside me.

"Looks dead to me," I said.

"We should say some words," Lula said. "It's only right that when you come on the deceased you say some words."

"You're going to pray over the groundhog?"

"He's God's creature."

"Okay. I get that."

We bowed our heads.

"Dear Lord," Lula said. "Bless this disgusting swelled-up groundhog and take him into the kingdom of heaven or wherever it is that dead groundhogs are supposed to go. Amen."

We both made the sign of the cross.

"I would have said more, but I didn't really know the deceased," Lula said.

I gave up a sigh. "You said enough. Let's go."

"Wait a minute," Lula said. "You can't leave him here. He could deface Ranger's car when you drive over him. He could explode and spray guts all over. And anyways it would be a waste. You should pick it up. You could feed it to Ethel."

"Are you crazy? I'm not picking it up!"

"Did you bring something else for Ethel to eat?"

"No."

"Well, then, you should bring her this groundhog. Otherwise you gotta go to the store and get Ethel some more rotisserie chicken."

I hated to admit it, but feeding the groundhog to Ethel wasn't an entirely bad idea. I was running out of rotisserie chicken money.

All Rangeman cars are equipped with emergency medical kits. I found disposable gloves for Lula and me, and a Mylar survival blanket we could use to protect the back of the Lexus. Lula and I pulled on gloves and returned to the groundhog. I spread the blanket out on the road and looked at Lula.

"I'll take the front legs, and you take the rear legs, and we'll put him on the blanket. Then we can carry him to the car."

"Ethel better appreciate this," Lula said. "I wouldn't do this for just any snake."

We grabbed the groundhog by his legs and dropped him onto the blanket.

"I think he's leaking something," Lula said. "It looks like gravy."

I gave a shudder and dragged the blanket to the SUV. We trundled the groundhog in, wrapped the blanket around him so no gravy would get on Ranger's car, and I closed the hatch. I drove about ten feet, and I got a call from Judy Chucci.

"He's here," she said. "The idiot is standing on my sidewalk holding a sign that says he loves me."

"I'm on my way," I told her. "Try to keep him there."

I made a U-turn and sped out of Diggery's neighborhood.

"What about Ethel?" Lula asked. "She's going to be wondering about breakfast."

"She has to wait. If I catch Johnny Chucci and bring him in, I can afford rotisserie chicken."

I cut across the Burg and reached Judy's street in record time. Her house was a block away, and I could see Johnny standing on the sidewalk with his sign.

"You gotta give him something for being persistent," Lula said. "Of course, aside from that he's a nutcase."

"I'm going to park and approach him. If he runs I'll go after him. You stay here and make sure he doesn't circle back and drive away. The silver Honda is parked across the street from Judy's house."

"No problem," Lula said. "I'll make sure he don't get near the car."

I pulled in behind the Honda, and Lula and I got out. Johnny didn't turn to look. He was waving his sign and watching for Judy to appear at the door. I guess he thought if he stayed there long enough she'd give in and come out. I was halfway across the street when he saw me. Recognition was instant. He dropped the sign and took off. I chased him between the two houses and through several backyards. He was surprisingly fast, hurdling over fences and crashing through hedges. I caught my toe on one of the fences and face-planted. I got up and continued to chase him, but I was far behind. He turned a corner, and by the time I got there he'd disappeared.

I stood still and listened. I didn't hear footsteps, but someone was breathing heavily not far away. At least I had the satisfaction of knowing he wasn't in any better shape than me.

"Hey, Johnny," I yelled. "Let's talk. I can help you."

I was at the corner, standing to one side of a shingled bungalow with a small front yard that had been cemented over and painted green. Johnny poked his head out from the other side.

"Go away. I'm not going to jail," he said.

"It could work out okay. Maybe the judge will be sympathetic, and you'll get off with community service."

"No way. I'll serve time and when I get out, Judy will be married. I'll never get her back."

"I don't think she's interested in you. I think you should move on."

"I can't," Johnny said. "I love her."

"Why?"

"I don't know. She's a stupid obsession. I can't stop thinking about her."

"Maybe you need a hobby. Prison might be a good thing. You could take up metalwork or pumping iron."

I moved toward him, and he jumped away from the house. "No!" he said. "Stay away from me. I have a gun."

"I don't see a gun."

"It's in my pocket."

"I want to see it."

Johnny struggled to get the gun out of his pocket, and *BANG!* He accidentally shot himself in the foot. He stared openmouthed at his foot for a couple beats, and fainted.

I called 911, and I called Lula. I elevated Johnny's feet, and was relieved when he opened his eyes.

"What?" he asked. "When?"

It took him a few minutes to fully come around and realize his foot hurt. I didn't bother with cuffs because he wasn't going to be running anywhere anytime soon. The gun was lying a safe distance away.

Lula drove up in Ranger's Lexus and parked. I could hear a fire truck a couple blocks away.

"What the heck?" Lula said, looking down at Johnny. "What'd the dumb ass do now?"

"Shot himself in the foot," I said.

"Well, that's nothing to be ashamed of," Lula said. "We've all been there."

Johnny was in a white-faced cold sweat. "Am I going to die?" he asked.

"Eventually, but not today," I told him. "You shot yourself in the foot. That's not usually fatal."

Ten minutes later the street was filled with first, second, and third responders. Johnny was strapped onto an EMT stretcher and rolled into the ambulance for the three-minute drive to St. Francis Medical Center. I rode with Johnny, and Lula took my car back to the office.

Johnny was admitted through the ER, and whisked away to prep for surgery, such as it was. If there were a lot of bones involved they might take him upstairs. Otherwise, the bullet would be removed down here, he'd get a shot of antibiotic, his foot would get bundled, and he'd get turned over to me. You wouldn't want to have brain surgery done at St. Francis, but you were in good hands with a gunshot. Emergency had lots of experience removing bullets.

It was actually a good time of day to get shot. Not a lot was going on in emergency, so the wait time for attention wasn't bad.

If he'd gotten shot at eleven at night he'd have to take a ticket and get in line.

After a half hour, I went back to check on Johnny. He was on an ER bed in one of the little draped cubicles. His shoe had been removed and his pants leg cut off at the knee. His foot was elevated and packed in ice.

"What's going on?" I asked him.

"I'm waiting for X-rays."

An ER doctor showed up and looked at the foot.

"Doesn't look terrible," he said.

"How long before he's discharged?" I asked.

"Are you his wife?"

"I'm a bail bonds apprehension agent, and he's a fugitive. When you're done with him he'll either be transferred upstairs to the lockup, or I'll take him downtown to the police station."

"I doubt he'll need to be hospitalized. His vitals are all okay, and I should be able to do this procedure under local anesthesia. With luck, he'll be out of here in a couple hours."

I returned to the waiting room and read all the magazines. I read my email. I spent time on Facebook. I got candy out of the vending machine and told myself it was lunch.

It was almost one o'clock when Johnny got rolled out of the back in a wheelchair. He was holding crutches and his discharge papers. He had a massive bandage around his foot, and he looked exhausted.

There was no way I could turn him in to the police. He looked pathetic.

"Is there someplace you can go for the night?" I asked him. "Your parents' house? One of your brothers'?"

"I thought I was going to jail."

"I can't take you in like this. They'll take your pain pills away, and you can't walk. I'll give you a couple nights to recover, but you have to promise not to leave the Burg."

"I promise. I guess I could stay with my parents."

"Great."

I called Lula and told her I needed a ride. Five minutes later she drove her red Firebird into the pick-up area just outside the ER. I helped Johnny into the back seat, handed him his crutches, and turned the wheelchair over to an aide.

"Are we going to the police station?" Lula asked.

"No," I said. "I'm going to let him stay with his parents for a couple nights."

Lula looked back at Johnny. "That's probably not smart, but it's nice. He looks done in."

She drove to the elder Chuccis' house, I helped Johnny to the door, and his mom took him in. She didn't look happy. Couldn't blame her.

"Where are we going now?" Lula asked.

"I should be looking for Slick, but I don't know where to begin."

"I got a theory," Lula said. "They haven't found any of his parts, right?"

"Right."

"I think that's because they turned him into a zombie, and he's hanging with the rest of them. You find the zombie pack, and you'll find Slick."

"That's a disturbing thought."

"You bet your ass. And it's a problem on account of zombies

don't like a lot of light so they skulk around in the shadows during the day. They could be holed up inside somewhere with the shades pulled down. And they could be watching MTV."

"Or they could have found a nice, dark building where Slick would be able to cook more meth."

"Exactly. Imagine a zombie on meth! That's epic crazy."

"I wasn't serious," I said.

"I get it. That was sarcasm. In my opinion that's not a healthy form of expression. It's filled with negativity. And anyways, I *was* serious. Something got Slick, and it makes sense it was the zombies."

"Assuming it was zombies, where would we find them?"

"Ordinarily I'd think to look in the cemetery, but they might have temporarily vacated it with all the cops roaming around."

"Any other ideas?"

"Diggery's woods. It's the perfect place for a bunch of zombies. And already we know they go there sometimes."

"Okay, do you want to go zombie hunting with me in Diggery's woods?"

"No. No way. No how. I don't think so. Not gonna happen. Also, I usually only work half a day on Saturday, and I'm past the halfway mark. I got an appointment to get my nails done this afternoon."

"No problem. Drop me at my car, and I'll see if I can talk Morelli into going with me."

"How about if I drop you at Morelli's house, and you'll be one step ahead of the game?"

"That won't work. I need my car so I can feed Ethel."

"About your car . . ." Lula said. "You know how it's such a nice sunny day?"

"Yeah."

"And you know how exceptionally warm it's got?"

"Yeah."

"And you know how a locked-up car can get overly hot inside when it's parked in the sun? Well, your car got parked in the sun, and the groundhog exploded."

"What?"

"Exploded. At least that's what we think happened. Hard to tell from what's left. Looked to Connie and me that you don't leave a dead groundhog in a hot car. Who would have thought?"

"Is it bad?"

"It isn't good," Lula said. "There's putrefied groundhog guts and gravy all over the place. I wouldn't want to be the one to detail it."

Lula eased to the curb behind my car, staying a good distance away.

"I need to park back here so I don't contaminate my baby with groundhog stink," she said.

"There are turkey vultures sitting on it."

"Yeah, we keep shooing them, but they keep coming back and pecking at the roof. I imagine you might have a few dents up there."

We got out of the Firebird and stood looking at the vultures.

"You want me to shoot them?" Lula asked.

"No."

I crept closer and looked inside.

"Omigod!" I said, clapping a hand over my mouth, holding my breath.

"It's like you exploded that sucker in a microwave, right? It's like when you forget to put the top on the blender. It's like projectile vomit from something possessed."

I bit into my lower lip to keep from whimpering. "Do you think it's totaled?"

"Not in the traditional sense of being flattened by a garbage truck or being run off a bridge into the Delaware, but in the sense that no one is gonna want to drive it . . . hell, yeah."

I closed my eyes and tried to calm myself. I'd destroyed yet another of Ranger's cars. And there was a bet riding on this. Double or nothing. I was in a relationship with Morelli, and I owed Ranger two nights. What was I thinking?

I called Ranger, and he answered with the usual "Babe."

"Bad news," I said. "It's about your Lexus."

"One of my patrol cars drove by it an hour ago and said it was being circled by vultures."

"There was an unfortunate incident with a dead groundhog."

"I didn't see that one coming," Ranger said. "How bad is it?"

"There are vultures circling. How bad do you think it is?"

Silence.

"You're laughing again, aren't you?" I asked him.

"Do I need to send someone in a hazmat suit?"

"Yes."

"Do you need another car? I'm running a tab."

"No. I don't need another car. I'm going to get Big Blue."

"Let me know if you change your mind."

Big Blue is a 1953 blue and white Buick Roadmaster in prime condition. My grandmother inherited it, and it now sits in my parents' garage and is available to borrow. It drives like a tank, and while some might think old cars are cool, I feel like an idiot in it. That said, it's free and comes with no strings attached.

"What's the plan?" Lula asked.

"Ranger is going to take care of the Lexus. I'm going to borrow Big Blue."

"I'll give you a ride. Then I'm going to get my nails done. I like my nails to be looking good. I get a chip in my nail varnish, and my juju goes in the dumper."

NINETEEN

GRANDMA OPENED THE door when I stepped onto the front porch. "We're done with lunch," she said, "but I can fix you a sandwich if you're hungry."

"Thanks. I've already eaten." Three Reese's Peanut Butter Cups, two Snickers bars, and a bag of M&M's. "I thought you had a date with Willie Kuber."

"It got over early. He got bursitis playing skillo. He was a dud anyway. All he could talk about was his prostate, and how he was getting radiation, and his prostate was going to turn into a useless leather hacky sack. I got an idea his prostate was useless before he got zapped."

"Bummer."

"Yeah. How are you doing with Johnny Chucci?"

"I captured him, but he shot himself in the foot, so I left him with his mother."

"Was he wearing his underpants on his head?"

"No."

"Too bad. I bet that would be something to see."

"I'm going to borrow Big Blue for a couple days."

"Help yourself. The keys are in the car."

I backed the Buick out of the garage and drove the short distance to Morelli's house. I let myself in and found Morelli in front of the television with a bag of chips and a beer. Bob was on the couch next to him.

"This game sucks," he said when he saw me. "Both teams suck."

I sat down at the far end of the couch and helped myself to some chips. I gave a couple to Bob and ate the rest.

"I need to feed Ethel," I said. "Want to ride shotgun?"

"Yeah. I live to feed Ethel."

"As a special bonus, you could look in the woods for zombies."

"Sorry. It's my day off from zombies."

I went to the kitchen and looked in his fridge. Half a leftover pepperoni pizza. Two boxes of frozen waffles in the freezer. A loaf of bread on the counter. I gathered them all up and put them in a grocery bag.

Morelli followed me. "What's with the food in the bag?"

"It's for Ethel. I'm out of rotisserie chicken money. I had some really great roadkill for her, but it exploded."

"I'm not even going to ask."

"I appreciate that, because I don't want to talk about it."

• • •

We took Morelli's car and drove down Diggery's road in silence, scanning the cleared areas and surrounding woods. We wouldn't admit to believing in zombies, but it was hard to dispute the presence of zombie-like *things.*

Morelli parked close to the double-wide, and I carefully entered and looked around. Ethel was coiled in the bedroom doorway.

"Hey!" I yelled. "Lunch."

I dumped the food on the dining table and returned to Morelli.

"How was it in there?" he asked, as I climbed into the front seat.

"Nothing new. How was it out here?"

"Lonely. Would you like to get naked?"

"Here?"

"Yeah. It's been a long time since we did it in a car."

"We never did it in a car."

"Are you sure?"

"Yes. You must be thinking of the hundreds, maybe thousands, of women you *did* in a car."

"We *almost* did it in a car."

"Yes. Almost."

He leaned across the gearshift and kissed me. His hand slid under my T-shirt and found my breast. His touch was warm and gentle. The first kiss was soft. The second kiss was pure passion. He unsnapped my bra, and his phone rang. We both froze. The phone kept ringing. Morelli yanked the phone out of his pocket and threw it out the window. The ringing stopped for a moment and then resumed.

"Probably you should answer it," I said. "It sounds official."

Morelli got out of the car and retrieved his phone. He had a short conversation and got back into the car.

"Well?" I asked.

"That was dispatch. Some woman claims she was chased out of her house by a zombie."

"Is this for real? Are you sure you aren't being punked?"

Morelli shrugged and rolled the engine over. "I'll know when I get there. She's on Surrey Street. That's two blocks from the Morley Street cemetery . . . the epicenter of zombie activity."

"I feel like I'm in a *Ghostbusters* movie."

"Yeah, this is a ten on the weird-o-meter. I find myself feeling nostalgic for the good old days when I was sticking to blood-soaked floors, investigating gang killings."

"After you talk to her, are you going to come home?"

"Yep."

"And then?"

"And then I'm going to make you happy," Morelli said.

"You're going to give me a back rub?"

"I'm going to rub every square inch of you."

Oh boy.

. . .

Morelli left me at his house and drove away. I didn't expect him to return anytime soon. He'd interview the woman and then get stuck at the station doing paperwork. I went to the kitchen and got a soda out of the fridge. I turned and bumped into Diesel.

"Jeez Louise," I said. "What the heck?"

"How's it going?" Diesel asked.

When I found my voice, it was an octave higher than normal. "What are you doing here?"

"Thought I'd stop in to say hello."

"You can't just pop into Morelli's house."

"Sure, I can. It's easy. His locks are crap." Diesel looked in the fridge. "There's nothing to eat in here."

"I gave the leftovers to Ethel."

"The snake? How's she doing?"

"She's doing okay."

Diesel looked in the cupboard and found a bag of pretzels. He helped himself to a beer and ate the pretzels.

"I like the pool table in the dining room," he said. "Nice touch."

"Where have you been?"

"Working. Looking for a guy."

"All day and night?"

"Whatever it takes," Diesel said, offering the pretzels to me.

I took a handful and got myself a beer. "Were you looking for him in the Morley Street cemetery?"

"Yeah. No luck."

"Don't suppose you want to tell me about it?"

"Not much to tell," Diesel said. "He's sort of a new age zombie."

"For real?"

Diesel shrugged. "As real as a zombie could get."

"The police have a video of you in the cemetery. It was taken by one of my FTAs. Zero Slick."

"Little guy? Brown ponytail?"

"Yes. He's disappeared."

"How'd they get the video if he disappeared?"

"He left his GoPro behind. Don't suppose you know where I can find him?"

"No. Maybe he's hanging with the zombies."

"Do you believe in zombies?"

"Honey pie, I believe in almost everything. Simplifies a lot of shit."

"You were there when the zombies attacked Slick," I said. "Why didn't you stop them?"

"They didn't attack him when I was there. I was tracking my target, and I passed a couple locals, but I didn't see any zombies."

"Their eyes were glowing in the video."

"Almost all eyes glow in infrared. There was probably a time lapse between frames that you didn't notice."

I grabbed another handful of pretzels. It was possible. Maybe.

"I thought you were supposed to be this super tracker," I said. "Why can't you find your guy?"

"He has his own skill set."

"Could you find Slick?"

"Slick isn't my problem."

"Yes, but he's *my* problem. And I could use some help."

Diesel grinned. "Maybe we could make a deal."

Omigod, another deal! Isn't it enough I have to sleep with Ranger? Okay, let's get real. I want to sleep with both these men. I mean, who wouldn't? Damnation. I was going straight to hell.

"What did you have in mind?" I asked.

"If I find him for you, I get to see you naked."

"That's it?"

"Should I have asked for more?"

"No!"

"I figure once you're naked . . . who knows."

I squinched my eyes closed and smacked myself in the forehead. *"Unh!"*

"Is that a yes?"

"No! It would feel icky to get naked and have you look at me."

"Okay, so how about strip poker?"

"No way. I've seen you play poker."

"You pick a game."

"Old Maid."

"Works for me. Let's go."

"Now?"

"Do you have something better to do?"

I followed him to the door. "Do you have a car? Do you know where to look?"

"Yes and no. Here's the way it works. You tell me where you want to look. We go there and walk around, and if he's there I'll probably know."

"I could do that."

"Yeah, but I can do it better. Where do you want to look?"

"His parents' house. The cemetery. The woods around Diggery's double-wide."

We stepped outside, I locked the door, and looked at the car parked behind Big Blue. It was a red Ferrari.

"That's your car?" I asked.

"It was available. I take what they give me."

"'They'?"

"My handlers."

I stared at him. "Who *are* you?"

"Diesel," he said. "Just Diesel."

"And that's another thing. Don't you have a last name?"

"It's Diesel, so you see the problem."

"You're Diesel Diesel?"

"My parents had a sense of humor not shared by the rest of the family. On the bright side, I have a cousin named Gerewulf Grimoire, so I suppose I should be happy."

He put his hand on the small of my back and moved me forward. I slid into the Ferrari and buckled up.

"Where would you like to go first?" he asked, settling behind the wheel.

Slick's parents were a long shot, and Morelli was most likely still in the vicinity of Morley Street, so I went with Diggery's woods.

Diesel drove down the single-lane road without looking side to side. He said it distracted from his radar. If anyone else said this I'd roll my eyes, but this was Diesel and what the heck, maybe he really had radar.

We parked in Diggery's yard at the end of the road and got out of the car. We stood very still and listened.

"Well?" I asked Diesel.

"It's quiet here. It's like it's not even Trenton. Wouldn't be half bad if it had some palm trees and a beach."

"There are a bunch of abandoned shelters tucked away in the woods. Cars, storage sheds, houses, tents. We could do a search of the area and see if any of these places are being used by . . . um, you-know-whats."

"Zombies?"

"Yes."

I wouldn't search the woods on my own. I'm not that brave, and I know my limitations. Even with Diesel I wasn't entirely comfortable snooping around. I'd been chased by dogs, and my car had been attacked by a zombie in Diggery's woods. And to make matters worse, I was operating without a pack of wieners.

"The road isn't that long," Diesel said. "A couple miles. We can walk down it and check out possible zombie dens."

"What will we do if we find zombies?"

"We'll ask them if they've seen Slick."

TWENTY

IT TOOK US an hour to reach the end of Diggery's road. Most of the houses had people living in them. The people didn't look all that great, but none of them looked like zombies. The dilapidated tents and yurts and sheds were also zombie free. We were almost back to Diggery's double-wide, and I realized we were at the bend in the road where I ran into the zombie. There were no houses here. It was heavily wooded on both sides, but now that I was on foot, I could see a path threading between the trees.

"I suppose we should see where that leads," I said to Diesel. "This is where I bounced the zombie off my right front quarter panel."

Diesel looked at me and grinned. "You ran over a zombie?"

"I didn't exactly run *over* him. He was in the middle of the road, and I kind of punted him to one side. By the time I got out of the car, he was gone."

"Honey, it's not good to piss off a zombie."

"That's what Lula said."

Diesel hugged me to him and kissed me on the top of the head. "This is getting to be fun."

Diesel followed the trail, and I followed Diesel. After a short walk, we came to a hole that had been dug in the ground. It was about six feet deep, and it looked like a tunnel opened off to one side. A ladder was propped against the wall of the hole.

Diesel jumped in and looked around.

"What's down there?" I asked.

"A tunnel. Mostly dirt shored up with some wood. Smells like dirt and carnations."

"Zombies!"

"Sweetheart, zombies only exist in Hollywood."

"I thought you said you believed in everything."

He looked up at me. "Rule number one. Never believe anything I tell you. I'm going to see where this tunnel leads. You want to come along?"

"No! How can you see in there? Do you have a flashlight?"

"I have good night vision."

"Am I supposed to believe that?"

"Your choice."

He disappeared into the tunnel, and I was left standing on the edge of the hole. I called down to Diesel, but he didn't answer. It was late afternoon, and it was getting dark under the tree canopy. I checked my email and slid my phone back into my pocket. I heard rustling behind me, turned, and came face-to-face with a zombie woman. Two men were behind her.

"I'd like your brain," she whispered to me.

Her face was smeared with dirt, and her hair was fright night. Her voice was six-packs-of-Camels-a-day raspy.

I stumbled back and almost fell into the hole. I yelled for Diesel, and then I took off. The zombies were in the path, so I ran through the woods in blind panic. I tripped and scraped my knee and my hands. I got up, listened for footsteps, and heard that they weren't far behind. I ran toward a patch of light and came out at Diggery's double-wide. I tried to get into the car, but it was locked. Diesel had the key. I ran for Diggery's front door, put my shoulder to it, and popped it open. I slammed the door shut and slid the bolt.

I was gasping for air, bent at the waist, and I saw Ethel looking at me. She was curled on the dining table.

"It's you and me against the zombies," I said to Ethel. "I'm counting on you."

There was banging on the door and some doorknob rattling. A moment of silence and then a rag-wrapped fist smashed through the window over the table. It broke the glass away, and a grotesque face looked in at me. Ethel raised her head and hissed at the face, and the face fell away.

God bless Ethel. I was going to bring her a leg of lamb tomorrow. A porterhouse steak. A ham.

I rummaged through Diggery's kitchen drawers and found a chef's knife. I went to his bedroom and searched for a gun. I found one under the bed. It was a long-barrel revolver, and it was loaded. Grandma had a similar gun.

I went back to Ethel and was about to dial Ranger when Diesel called.

"I'm outside," he said. "Open the door."

"I thought you had this mysterious ability to open doors."

"I didn't want to startle the snake."

"You don't like snakes?"

"Not my favorite."

I opened the door and looked past Diesel to the woods, checking for red eyes.

"What's with the gun and the knife?" he asked. "Are you planning to shoot the snake?"

"I was chased through the woods by three zombies. I couldn't get into the car, so I locked myself in here and borrowed Diggery's gun."

His eyes focused on the broken window. "Has that window always been broken?"

"No. One of the zombies put his fist through it. Ethel hissed at him, and he went away."

"And you think they were zombies?"

"For lack of a better word."

"Notice anything significant about the window?"

My breathing was almost back to normal, and my voice had stopped shaking. I looked over at the broken window. "Blood," I said. "The zombie got cut when he smashed the glass. Unusual for a zombie to bleed."

"Unheard-of," Diesel said.

I put the gun and the knife back where I found them. We left the double-wide and got into the car.

"What did you find in the tunnel?" I asked Diesel.

"It was more cave than tunnel. It looked like it originally

might have been a root cellar. There was a burned-down cabin not far away. The cabin isn't habitable, but someone's recently used the cave."

"The zombies."

"Yeah, the zombies. They've been doing new digging. There was a decomposed head partially covered with dirt, and I think I saw what might be foot bones. I didn't do a lot of exploring. Didn't want to disturb the crime scene. You should call it in to Morelli. And tell him to have CSI check out the bloody window glass."

I dialed Morelli, and he answered on the first ring.

"I went back to Diggery's," I said. "I did some exploring and found a hole in the ground that looks like it leads somewhere. You need to check it out. I was standing over it and three zombies appeared out of nowhere and chased me back to Diggery's double-wide. One of the zombies smashed a window trying to get at me, but Ethel scared him away."

"Where are you now? Are you okay?"

"I'm fine. Just a little freaked. I'm heading back to your house. Where are you?"

"I'm at the station, doing paperwork."

"You want to take CSI with you to Diggery's. The zombie cut himself when he smashed the window, and he left a blood smear."

"Zombies don't bleed," Morelli said.

"Exactly. About a quarter mile before you get to the double-wide, there's a bend in the road. If you look right you'll see a path going into the woods. Follow the path to the zombie den."

"I'm on it."

"How did it go with the woman who got chased out of her house?"

"She was in her kitchen, and a zombie walked in and told her he wanted her brain. She said he was filthy and his eyes were red, but he was surprisingly short for a zombie. She said he had a brown ponytail and looked confused."

"Do you think it could have been Slick?"

"I guess it's possible. Ziggy was first on the scene, and he said there was no sign of the intruder. They cleared the house, but the woman was too upset to stay there. She's spending the night with her sister."

Diesel waited for me to end the call.

"We should be moving out if the police are moving in," he said.

• • •

We drove to Morley Street and cruised the neighborhood. Houses and lots were larger here than in the Burg. Not palatial mansions, but comfortable family homes that had more than one bathroom. There was no police presence in the area. Presumably they had all moved over to Diggery's dirt road.

"It all looks so normal," I said to Diesel. "Hard to believe there are zombies roaming around."

Diesel pulled into the cemetery lot and parked. "Let's look around," he said. "I didn't get a chance to see much last time I was here."

We walked through the gate and followed the main path. "Do you think the guys you saw could have been zombies?" I asked Diesel.

"They weren't zombies when I saw them. They were just hanging out, smoking weed. The south side of the cemetery, by the church and Morley Street, is well maintained. The north side backs up to the projects. It's littered with trash and discarded drug paraphernalia."

We stopped at Slick's campsite and looked around. It was clear that the grave had been exhumed. Nothing else seemed out of the ordinary. All traces of police activity had been removed. There weren't any signs warning people of a zombie portal.

"What do you think?" I asked Diesel. "Are you getting any ideas?"

"Yeah, but none that relate to zombies."

I raised an eyebrow. "What then?"

"Bacon cheeseburger."

"Anything else?"

"Onion rings, fries, beer."

"Does that mean we're done here?" I asked him.

"No. It means we need to keep walking. There's a burger place just before you get to the projects."

"Mickey's," I said. "I've been there. They have excellent cheese fries."

We wandered off the path, covering as much of the cemetery as possible, but we found no new dig sites. We exited through the gate just before the projects and crossed the street to

Mickey's. I'd been there a bunch of times before with Lula. Lula could sniff out cheese fries a mile away.

Mickey's consisted of a small, windowless room with four booths on one side and a bar on the other. It was so dark the booths could have been occupied by zombies, tree fairies, or gorillas and no one would know. It smelled like burgers and beer and deep fried everything. We slid into a booth and ordered.

"What's the deal with you and Morelli?" Diesel asked. "You've been seeing him off and on for how long? Thirty years?"

"Not thirty."

"Does it seem like thirty?"

"Is this going somewhere?" I asked him.

"Just curious."

"What's the longest relationship you've ever had?"

"Forty-eight hours," Diesel said. "I thought it would never end."

"Seriously."

A pitcher of beer was delivered, and we both chugged some down.

"Define 'relationship,'" Diesel said. "Does it involve cohabitation? Is it sexual? Is love involved? Do you have to share a bathroom?"

"Pick any two out of those four things."

"Then you're probably one of my longer relationships . . . off and on."

"Is your mother upset about this?"

"My mother is a strange woman."

No doubt.

The bartender brought our burgers, fries, and onion rings to the table, and we dug in. I finished my burger and called Morelli while I picked at the cheese fries.

"Just checking in," I said to him. "Are you finding anything?"

"CSI is at work in the pit. You said you saw three zombies here, correct?"

"Yes."

"We've sealed off as much as we can, and we're combing the woods. Unfortunately, we're hampered by the dark."

"Did you get a blood sample from the broken glass?"

"Yes. And I had someone board the window up, so Ethel doesn't sneak out. I've got thirteen men searching the woods. None of them wants to get friendly with Ethel."

"When do you think you'll get back to the house?"

"At this rate, it'll be Tuesday."

I disconnected and gave up a sigh.

"Honey," Diesel said, "you need a man you can count on."

"Like you?"

"No. I make Morelli look good. I'm fun, but I'm not someone you'd want to count on."

"Good to know."

Diesel grinned and paid the check. "Let's go for a walk through a cemetery."

It was dark when we left the bar. The sky was overcast with just a hint of moon low on the horizon. There was traffic on the street behind us, but the cemetery in front of us was deathly silent.

We went a short distance on the path, and Diesel stopped.

"Do you smell that?" he asked.

"Yes, but I don't know what it is. It reminds me of an electrical fire I had in one of my cars. And at the same time, it's sweet."

"Like carnations."

"Oh crap. Zombies?"

He took my hand and tugged me forward. "Let's go say hello."

Diesel left the path and cut across several graves to an aboveground crypt. I could make out two figures huddled next to the crypt. They appeared to be heating something in a metal measuring cup with a large Bic-type lighter. They saw us approach, and they extinguished the lighter.

"Back off," one of them said to us. "Or die."

"We're looking for Slick," Diesel said.

"Look someplace else. There's no Slick here."

"What's in the cup?" Diesel asked.

The guy holding the lighter pulled a gun and fired. In the next instant, he had a knife stuck in his eye. It happened so fast I didn't see the knife thrown. He screamed and fell back, dropping the gun. The other guy tossed the cup, grabbed his friend, and they scrambled away into the shadows. The cup hit the ground with a splash of iridescent green and a hiss of steam.

I almost lost my burger and fries. One second I was terrified that I'd get shot, and the next I was dumbstruck at the sight of the knife stuck in the gunman's eye. I clapped my hands over my mouth and swallowed back the horror.

"Holy cow!" I said. "How did you do that? Where did the knife come from?"

"Reflex action," Diesel said. "I have a strong sense of survival."

"Did you mean to put it in his eye?"

"Lucky throw," Diesel said.

I didn't believe it was a lucky throw. I thought it was an accurate throw.

Diesel played the light from his iPhone over the patch of grass where the cup had landed, but there was no remnant of the cup's contents. Only the lingering scent of carnations.

"Morelli might like to see this measuring cup," Diesel said.

I took a tissue from my messenger bag and used it to pick the cup up.

"What do you think was in this?" I asked.

"Probably a street drug. Difficult to see in the dark, but I've been through here before, and there are discarded syringes in this area."

"A street drug that turns people into zombies? Something similar to bath salts?"

Diesel stared at me for a beat, and moved toward the path. "Time to head out."

I stayed close to him on the way back to the car. There were some far-off, eerie moaning sounds, but I didn't suggest that we investigate. I didn't know how many secret weapons Diesel carried, and I didn't want to risk another knife in the eye episode. I was barely holding on to my cheese fries.

Diesel was wearing a long-sleeved black T-shirt untucked with the sleeves pushed up to his elbow. We got into the car, and I realized his right sleeve had a tear in it and was soaked with blood.

"You're bleeding!" I said.

"It isn't serious. The bullet grazed my arm. Hard to believe he could be such a bad shot at such close range."

"We should get you to a doctor."

"Not necessary. I'm a good healer. I'm going to drop you at Morelli's, and then I'll stop off at your place to get a clean shirt. I still have work to do tonight."

"Would you like some help?"

"Thanks for the offer, but I have to do this alone."

Diesel was silent for the rest of the drive. I had the measuring cup on the floor by my feet, and I was trying to think of something other than the knife in the guy's eye and the blood on Diesel's shirt. I conjured up the sand and surf of Long Beach Island, my mom's pineapple upside-down cake, and Ranger naked. I thought about kittens and puppies and grilled cheese sandwiches. I was cycling back to Ranger naked when Diesel pulled to the curb in front of Morelli's house.

He walked me to the door, leaned in, and kissed me. Friendly. No tongue. No groping. A little disappointing.

"I'll catch up with you tomorrow," he said. "Keep your doors locked."

I nodded yes, stepped back, closed and locked the door. Bob galloped into the foyer, slamming into me, almost taking me to the floor. I told him he was a good boy, and we danced into the kitchen. I set the cup on a paper towel in the kitchen, and let him out to tinkle or do whatever in the backyard. I kept a watch for red eyes.

I filled Bob's bowl with dog kibble and gave him fresh water.

Two hours later we were both asleep on the couch, in front of the television, when Morelli came home.

Bob awoke first. He was off the couch when the door opened. I was slower to come out of the sleep fog. Morelli hugged Bob and ruffled his ears. He leaned down and kissed me. Friendly. No tongue. No groping. What the hell?

Morelli shuffled into the kitchen and got a beer out of the fridge. "I'm beat," he said. "I'm getting too old for this overtime crap. I'm ready to go back to being a uniform."

I followed after him. "You don't mean that."

"No. But I'm flat-out done."

"Did you catch any zombies?"

"We came close, but no. They were there. We could smell them. Carnations and rot. They must have another den somewhere in the woods. We'll go back tomorrow when it's light." He spotted the measuring cup on the counter. "What's this?"

"I went to the cemetery on Morley Street to look for Slick, and stumbled across two guys who were cooking something in this cup. They tossed the cup when they saw me and ran away. Whatever was in the cup glowed iridescent green and evaporated. Poof. There were a bunch of syringes lying around. I think this is some new street drug. And it occurred to me that it might be like the drug bath salts. Maybe something that makes people think they're zombies."

"Flakka?" he asked.

"Maybe a derivative of flakka," I said.

"I'll have CSI take a look at it. As it is, they're working

overtime. You can't imagine what we found in the hole in Diggery's woods."

"Bones? Brains?"

"No brains. Everything else." Morelli got a bag of chips out of the cupboard. "Talk to me about the cemetery. You went there alone?"

"Do you remember Diesel?"

"Big guy. Blond hair. Makes Ranger look normal."

"Yeah. He was with me."

"Do I want to know about this?"

"Nothing to tell. I'm letting him stay in my apartment since I'm here with you. He's never in town for long."

Morelli looked at the measuring cup. "So these guys just ran away?"

"Yep."

"And whatever was in this evaporated?"

"Yes. It went *hissss* and evaporated. Okay, actually the one pulled a gun and shot Diesel. But it was just a nick. And then Diesel threw a knife that got stuck in the guy's eye. And then they ran away."

"Are you kidding me?"

"No. That's the way it happened. I almost threw up. The knife was sticking out of his eye."

"You could have a nice safe job stacking oranges at the grocery store. You could get a job at the button factory. Is it really necessary that you continue to be a bounty hunter?"

"You sound like my mother."

Morelli put the chips back. "I'm too tired to eat these."

We trudged upstairs, and Morelli headed for the bathroom.

"I'm going to take a fast shower," he said. "Feel free to get started without me."

"I thought you were tired."

"Cupcake, I'm never *that* tired."

TWENTY-ONE

I WAS IN the kitchen, waiting for the coffee maker to dispense my coffee, when Morelli and Bob came in from their Sunday morning run. Hard to say which looked worse. Bob with his tongue hanging out of his mouth or Morelli dripping sweat.

"Looks like you guys had fun," I said.

"Yeah, I love these Sunday morning runs," Morelli said.

"What's the plan for the day?"

"I promised Anthony I'd help him put in a new tub. He's renovating his bathroom."

Anthony is Morelli's brother. He's been married a couple times to the same woman. They have a pack of kids. And if I had to give an honest description of him I'd say he's a likable asshole. The tub will probably take an hour to install, but Morelli will be gone all day. Anthony's house is a black hole. Morelli will get sucked into playing ball with his nephews, drinking beer with his brother, and by afternoon the house will be filled with guys from the neighborhood watching the game on Anthony's big flat-screen.

Bob flopped onto the floor, panting and drooling, and Morelli went upstairs to change. When Morelli returned to the kitchen, Bob had stopped panting and I was on my second coffee. Morelli's hair was still damp from his shower. He was wearing a T-shirt and jeans, and it was Sunday, so he hadn't shaved. Morelli with a day-old beard looked sexy and sinister.

Bob went with Morelli, and I went back to my apartment to feed Rex and get clean clothes. I didn't see Diesel's Ferrari in my parking lot when I drove in. Probably out looking for his man.

I entered the building, stepped into the elevator, and pressed the button for the second floor. I got a chill when the doors closed, and I caught the lingering odor of dirt and carnations. The elevator doors opened, and I looked out at the hall. Empty. No zombies. Just the same sickening stench. A flash of panic ripped through me when I got to my apartment. Someone or something had scratched *brains* and *die* into the paint on my door. And there was a red smear across the door and on the knob. I suspected it was blood.

The door was still locked, so at least they hadn't been able to get inside. I opened it, stepped in, and called, "Hello?" No one answered. I had a gun in my cookie jar, but I didn't have any bullets. I had a couple steak knives in my kitchen, but I couldn't see myself sticking one in someone's eye. And I was all out of brave. I grabbed Rex's cage off the kitchen counter, locked my apartment, and used my phone to take a picture of the mess.

I hustled down the stairs and out to Big Blue. I had a dilemma now. Where should I go? I didn't want to go to my parents' house if I was being stalked by a brain eater. They had enough problems managing Grandma. No reason to add some pseudo-zombie sneaking around, trying to get into their house.

I needed to show the picture to Morelli, but I didn't want to ruin his Sunday. I was afraid he'd feel compelled to abandon Anthony and go over every square inch of my hall with CSI. I also didn't want to hang out in Morelli's house all by myself. I supposed I could spend the day at Anthony's, watching the bathtub get installed, but, honestly, I'd rather have my brain sucked out by one of the zombies.

I had no idea how to get in touch with Diesel. He came and went like the wind. He gave me cellphone numbers that never worked. His cars had phony license plates. And I wasn't sure what he could do for me anyway.

That left the Holiday Inn or Ranger's. I didn't have money for the Holiday Inn, so it was going to be Ranger's. He lived in a one-bedroom apartment on the seventh floor of his high-security office building. I've stayed there before when I needed a safe haven.

I called Ranger, and he answered with his usual "Babe."

"I've got a situation here," I said. "I was wondering if Rex and I could hang out at Rangeman for a short time."

"How short?"

"Anywhere from a couple hours to a couple days."

"I'm in North Carolina with a client. I probably won't be back in town until midweek or later, but I'll notify the control room that you're on your way. You know the drill."

"I do. Thanks."

I drove into the center of the city and turned onto a side street that was mostly residential. Ranger's building is a discreet redbrick midrise that blends in with the rest of the neighborhood. The underground parking is gated and patrolled.

I flashed my card at the gate, watched it roll away, and drove through. Ranger's reserved parking is at the back, next to the elevator. The rest of the garage houses employee vehicles and the Rangeman fleet. I parked in one of Ranger's spaces, hauled Rex out of the back seat, and stepped into the elevator. I looked up at the security camera and smiled hello. I slid my card into a slot by the door, and the elevator took me to Ranger's private floor.

His apartment is professionally decorated in blacks and browns. Walls are white. It's uncluttered to the point of being impersonal. The furniture is sleek and comfortable. His sheets are two hundred thread count. His bathroom has fluffy white towels and Bulgari shower gel. His kitchen is small but well stocked. His housekeeper sees to it all.

I let myself in and walked down the short hall to the kitchen. I put Rex on a section of countertop and gave him fresh water, a shelled walnut from a bag in the cupboard, and fruit salad from the fridge. Ranger eats healthy.

I felt comfortable knowing everyone was safe. Rex was safe. Morelli and Bob were safe. My parents and Grandma were safe.

I'd removed myself from all those places. If a zombie was out there looking for me and my brain, he'd have no reason to disturb anyone I loved.

I watched Rex take his food out of his food cup and put it into his soup-can nest. After he had all his food stored away, he burrowed into his bedding material and disappeared. Okay, that was fun, but now I had nothing to do. I could go to the mall. I could go to the shore. I could take a nap.

I was leaning toward the nap when my mom called.

"Your grandmother is missing," she said. "I came home from church, and no one was home."

"Where's Dad?"

"He's at the lodge working a pancake breakfast. The man won't butter his own bread at home, but he's all about making pancakes at the lodge."

"Grandma goes out all the time."

"She left me a note. She said she was going to see her honey. And her suitcase isn't in the attic with the rest of the suitcases. I think she's going to Florida. I tried calling her, but she won't answer."

Oh boy. Grandma and the swingers.

"I was only gone for an hour and a half," my mother said. "You might be able to catch her at the airport."

"Which airport? What airline?"

"The one that goes to Florida," my mother said.

"The Trenton airport has flights to Florida, but they're limited. If Grandma is trying to get to Florida, she'll probably fly out of Newark. So how will she get to Newark?"

"Myra Rulach or Ester Nelley. All her other friends have had their licenses confiscated."

"Call them and see if they took Grandma to the airport."

Ten minutes later my mom called back. "Ester Nelley took her to Newark Airport and dropped her off at United. You have to go get her."

"Why me?"

"If I send your father he'll personally put her on the plane. And I can't go because I already took two Valium and had a calming cocktail."

"It's not even noon! And no one's died."

"Special circumstances," my mother said. "I felt a migraine coming on. Anyway, you don't have to live with this woman. You don't know what it's like. Last month she ran up a seventy-five-dollar bill on adult television. She said she was doing research on monkeys spanking fraternity men."

Sick and yet disturbingly intriguing.

"Okeydokey then," I said, "I'll see if I can find Grandma."

I drove Big Blue out of Ranger's garage and took Route 1 to the turnpike. There wasn't a lot of traffic at this time on a Sunday, but even with light traffic it wasn't a great drive. Needless to say, I was the only one on the road in a powder blue and white Buick Roadmaster. I took the turnoff to the airport and parked in short-term parking. I ran into the United terminal and didn't see Grandma.

I called my mom. "I'm at the airport, and I don't see her," I said. "A plane left for Miami twenty minutes ago. Call Ester back and see if Grandma was planning on taking that plane."

I sat in one of the waiting areas and cringed when my mom called back.

"Ester said your grandmother was hoping to make the plane that just left. And then she was making connections for Key West."

Great. Key West. It might as well be the moon.

I went to the ticket counter and got a ticket on the next flight out. It left at four-thirty and got into Miami at seven-thirty. The connecting Key West flight was at eight o'clock. Personally, I felt like Grandma was capable of taking care of herself, and if she wanted to go to Key West she should go to Key West. On the other hand, my mom was popping Valium and swilling down whiskey. And the spanking monkeys were troublesome. There was a small fear that Grandma would be romping around on a nude beach doing nooners with the swingers. I was no one to judge, but there were diseases to worry about.

I walked around the airport, ate a turkey wrap for lunch, and called Morelli.

"Did you get the bathtub in?" I asked him.

"Yeah. It looks good. Rooney came over and hooked up the plumbing."

"And now?"

"Now we're grilling burgers and sausages. You should come over."

"Rain check. I'm in Newark Airport. Grandma decided to go to Florida to hook up with Mr. Wrong, so I've been dispatched to bring her back. I'm one flight behind her."

"How do you know it's Mr. Wrong?"

"I ran a background on him. He's married, and he belongs to a swingers club."

"There are still swingers clubs? I thought they went the way of the phone booth."

"This one is in Key West."

"I guess that explains some of it," Morelli said. "How long do you expect to be in Florida?"

"No longer than necessary. My hope is that I'll catch up with Grandma at the connecting flight. If I get to her in time we might be able to make a nine o'clock plane back to Newark. If I don't get to her in time, I'll have to hunt her down in Key West."

"What if Grandma doesn't want to come home?"

"I'll bribe her with a puppy."

"Sounds like a plan," Morelli said. "Good luck."

I checked my email and Facebook page, ate a bag of M&M's, and dozed in the waiting area until my plane boarded. There were a lot of strange people in the airport, but none that looked like a zombie. So it was all good.

The flight was uneventful, and we landed on time. I went to the gate for the Key West connection and found Grandma on a bench in the lounge.

"For goodness' sakes," she said when she saw me. "This is a surprise. Are you going to Key West? I didn't know you were planning a trip."

"Mom was worried about you and sent me to make sure you were okay."

"Of course, I'm okay. I'm just dandy. My Key West boyfriend invited me to a party at his seniors club."

Eeeek. "I need to talk to you about that club."

"He said they had some fun activities, and I figured since Willie Kuber turned out to be a dud I might as well see what Roger Murf is about."

"I got the background check on Murf. He's married. And the seniors club is for swingers."

"The married part is a disappointment," Grandma said. "Did you get a picture?"

I pulled the photo out of my messenger bag and handed it over to her. "The woman is his wife, Miriam."

Grandma studied the photo. "He's no George Hamilton."

"Only George Hamilton is George Hamilton."

Grandma nodded. "George Hamilton is a good-looking man. This Roger Murf isn't doing it for me. And since Roger Murf is one of those swingers, I'm thinking he only wanted me for my body," Grandma said.

"He wanted you for Mom's body."

"Technically that's true, but a senior citizens' swingers club might not be too picky. I bet I could pull it off. I might have to get one of them Brazilian wax jobs. I hear they're painful. And when they're done with you, you're bald down there."

"How about a puppy? Why don't we go home and get a puppy?"

"That would beat the heck out of a swingers party," Grandma said.

"Okay, it's settled. If we hurry, we can get back to United in time for a flight to Newark and then we can get the puppy first thing in the morning."

"I'm going to name him Henry," Grandma said.

. . .

It was after midnight when we deplaned in Newark. The airport shops and restaurants were closed, and the corridors were mostly empty. Grandma had a small carry-on bag, and I had nothing other than my messenger bag. We bypassed the checked baggage carousels and walked through the terminal directly to short-term parking. I found Big Blue and was confronted with the reality that I'd parked in short-term all day. Between the airfare and the parking, it had been a costly night. And tomorrow I was going to have to buy Grandma a puppy!

It was a long, quiet drive in the dark back to Trenton. I'd texted my mom and told her I was bringing Grandma home. I didn't tell her about the puppy.

Lights were still on in my parents' house when I pulled to the curb. My mom was waiting up for Grandma.

"Thanks for going all that ways to tell me about the Murfs," Grandma said. "It's probably just as well I didn't go to the party. I don't know if I want to look at a bunch of naked old people. It would be different if it was those Chippendales men."

I waited until Grandma was safely inside, and then I headed over to Morelli's neighborhood. I drove down his street and idled in front of his house. It was dark. I hadn't called him, and he wasn't expecting me. Not that it mattered. I had a key.

I parked Big Blue at the curb, let myself in, and started to tip-toe up the stairs when Bob came bounding down and slammed into me. So much for my stealth entrance.

Morelli was at the head of the stairs. He was naked, and he had a gun.

"I wasn't expecting you," Morelli said.

"I see you're armed and dangerous."

He looked down at himself. "It's going to get a lot more dangerous now that you're here."

TWENTY-TWO

I HEARD MORELLI calling me through the fog of sleep. His hand was on my bare shoulder. I think he kissed me on the forehead. Or maybe I was dreaming.

"Steph!"

I opened my eyes. "Again?"

"No," Morelli said. "I have to go to work, but I need to show you something first."

"What time is it?"

"Six o'clock."

"In the morning?" I sat up and swung my legs over the side of the bed. "This better be good. I hope you're not going to show me the same stuff you showed me last night."

Morelli grinned. "You liked it last night."

"Yes, but that was last night. I'm not a morning person." I looked around for my clothes. "Should I get dressed?"

Morelli grabbed a robe from the closet, stuffed me into it, and tied the belt. "This will only take a minute," he said. "And then you can go back to bed."

I followed him down the stairs to the front door and stared at the words scratched into it: NEED BRAIN. Below it was the stick figure of a woman with curly hair. A half-empty take-out container and plastic fork had been left in the middle of Morelli's sidewalk.

"What's with the trash?" I asked.

"Zombie late-night snack," Morelli said. "The deli label says 'calf brains,' and I'm not sure, but it looks like it was doused with hot sauce."

He took a plastic evidence bag from his pocket and gingerly dropped the take-out container and fork into it.

"How could the zombie have known I was here?" I asked.

"Maybe it didn't. Maybe this was random."

"I don't think it was random. When I went back to my apartment yesterday, 'brains' and 'die' had been scratched into my door. There was a smear of something that looked like blood. And the elevator smelled like carnations."

"You didn't tell me."

"I didn't want to ruin your day."

"Nice of you, but misguided."

"It would be good if you could figure this out and get rid of the zombies."

"I should start to get the lab reports back today. Plus, I'm going back to Diggery's woods with a search team. In the meantime, you need to be careful. Keep the doors locked. And I can't believe I'm saying this, but put some bullets in your gun."

"Did the zombie write anything on my car?"

"It looks like it tried but couldn't scratch through the paint."

"If you're going back to Diggery's woods, I'd appreciate it if you'd feed Ethel. She'll eat almost anything. Pizza, burgers, rotisserie chicken, roadkill."

Morelli grimaced, kissed me goodbye, and waited for me to go inside and lock the door. I watched him drive away, and I looked down at Bob.

"No way am I going back to bed," I said. "I'm not taking a shower here, either. I'm moving out."

I picked my clothes up off the bedroom floor and put them on. I made the bed. And I made a fast stop in the kitchen for a bag of dog food.

"Don't worry," I said to Bob, hooking him up to his leash. "I'm not leaving you here. Bob brain isn't going to be on the zombie menu."

We piled into Big Blue, and I drove to the office. It was a little after seven o'clock, and no one was there. The office didn't open until eight o'clock.

"No problem," I said to Bob. "We need breakfast anyway."

I drove past the office to the Cluck-in-a-Bucket drive-thru. I ordered two Clucky Lucky Breakfast Meals and a large coffee. I picked up the food and parked in the lot. The breakfast meal included an egg and cheese sandwich on an English muffin, home fries that had been compressed into something resembling a deck of cards, and a mystery pastry.

Bob snarfed his food down in about fifteen seconds. I ate at a slightly more leisurely pace, but even at that, I still had some time to kill. I returned to the bonds office, parked the car, and walked Bob until Connie showed up and unlocked the front door. Lula was minutes behind her.

"What's with Bob?" Lula asked. "You don't usually hang with him."

"It's complicated," I said. "The short version is that I don't feel comfortable leaving him in Morelli's house alone."

"What about your house?" Connie asked. "What about your parents' house?"

"Even worse."

"Is this about the zombies?" Lula asked. "Are they eating dog brains now? I've been doing research, and zombies can't see real good with their red eyes, but they got a class A nose . . . unless it's been rotted away. I don't know what zombies do when their nose rots away. Anyway, if they have a nose, they can track you down by your scent, so all you have to do is smell different. I'm thinking about going into business making anti-zombie stink spray. It would be a combination of smells to confuse a zombie. Like cucumber and cat pee. Or maybe cow sweat and licorice. Stuff like that, you see what I'm saying? I bet I could clean up on stink spray."

"No one is going to want to smell like cucumber and cat pee," I said.

"Well, I guess people gotta make up their mind if they want their brains sucked out by a zombie, or if they want to smell like one of my designer stink sprays," Lula said. "I'm going into production as soon as I can find the right spray nozzle. I already got a source for cucumbers and cat pee."

"If you come into the office smelling like cucumber and cat pee you're out of a job," Connie said.

"I don't need to personally wear it right now anyway," Lula said, "because I'm not being pursued by a zombie, but there's others probably be happy to pay top dollar for it. Especially those individuals who are zombiephobics. Like if you have a business and you don't want to sell your product to a zombie, all you have to do is douse your shop in my stink spray. Zombies will be going someplace else to shop, and no one's going to protest your establishment, and the government isn't going to come near you and force you to sell to zombies. It's genius, right?"

Connie and I nodded. Lula was a lunatic. And yet, she could be on to something.

"I need to go to my apartment to get some things," I said to Lula. "How about riding shotgun?"

"Sure, I could do that," Lula said. "I imagine you want me to shoot any zombies who might pop up."

"Only if they try to get my brain," I said.

• • •

Lula and Bob trooped into my apartment building with me, and we all took the elevator to the second floor. The elevator no longer smelled like carnations. The hall was empty. My door was still vandalized.

"Look at here," Lula said. "Some zombie has no sense of respecting personal property. These are deep scratches. Someone's going to have to sand this down and repaint it. You

215

should find the zombie that did this and make him pay for the repairs."

"I'm working on it," I said, unlocking my door.

Bob pushed past me and ran around, jumping on furniture and snuffling rugs. Lula stayed in the small foyer.

"Where's Rex?" she asked. "I don't see his cage in the kitchen."

"He's having a sleepover at Rangeman."

"Lucky him," Lula said.

I went to my bedroom and stuffed some clothes into a medium-sized duffel bag. I added my laptop. It took me two minutes max, and I was ready to vacate. Truth is, I was much more frightened of a human pseudo-zombie than I would be of a real zombie. A Hollywood zombie would have to live by zombie rules. A pseudo-zombie would be unpredictable and have human emotions and obsessions . . . like needing a specific brain, as opposed to any old brain. Like maybe needing *my* brain.

On my way out, I checked for Diesel's knapsack. Still there. My bed had been slept in and a towel was damp in the bathroom. I felt a sense of relief, because it meant Diesel was okay.

"What are we doing now?" Lula asked.

"We're going to check on Johnny Chucci, and then I'm taking Grandma shopping."

"What kind of shopping?"

"Grandma's getting a puppy."

"Say what?"

"It's complicated."

"You say that a lot. Am I going along to get this puppy?"

"No. You're going to babysit Bob at the office."

Lula turned in her seat and looked at Bob.

"I guess I could do that, as long as I don't have to take him for a walk and pick up his poop."

"No problem," I said. "He's already been for a walk. He'll be happy to take a nap."

I turned off Hamilton, wound around the maze of streets in the Burg, and parked in front of Johnny's parents' house. I left Lula and Bob in the car, and I went to the small front porch and rang the bell. Mrs. Chucci answered.

"I came to see how Johnny is doing," I said to Mrs. Chucci.

"He's doing much better," she said. "He moved out yesterday."

"Moved out? Where did he go?"

"He had a reconciliation with his ex-wife."

"She had a restraining order against him."

Mrs. Chucci nodded. "Life is strange, isn't it? I suppose she realized she still had feelings for him when he got shot."

I thanked Mrs. Chucci and went back to Big Blue.

"Well?" Lula asked. "How's he doing?"

"He's doing great. He's back with his ex-wife."

"You mean he's standing on the street with a sign again?"

"I don't know."

. . .

I cut across the Burg and parked in front of Judy Chucci's house. I didn't see Johnny hobbling around on the sidewalk, so I assumed he was inside. I went to the door and rang the bell. No answer. I looked in the window. The house was dark. Wall to wall gnomes. No one walking around. I went to the back door. I knocked. I looked in the window. Lots of gnomes. No people. Door locked. I went back to the car.

"No one home," I said to Lula.

"Maybe they killed each other, and they're dead. You should bust in and take a look," Lula said.

I had authority as a bail bonds agent to break into a house if I felt my felon was inside. I used this privilege only under extreme circumstances. It was dangerous, and I wasn't especially talented at kicking a door down. In this case, I also couldn't get excited about finding two dead people. Or, for that matter, destroying a window or a door only to discover that Judy and Johnny were out grocery shopping.

"Hang for a little while longer," I said to Lula. "I'm going to talk to the neighbor."

Houses on either side of Judy Chucci's were normal. Small patches of grass that served as front yards. Neatly maintained. No gnomes.

I rang the bell on the house to the left of Judy's, and a young woman came to the door with a baby under her arm.

"I'm looking for Judy," I said. "She's not answering her door, and the house looks deserted. Have you seen her lately?"

"She left early this morning," the woman said. "She got back together with her fruitcake ex-husband, and they went on a pre-re-wedding honeymoon. She came over and asked me to take care of her gnomes. She said the one with the bad eye was feeling anxious about the fruitcake moving back in."

"Do you know where they went?"

"Hawaii."

I went back to Lula and Bob and took a deep breath. I was in financial doo-doo. I'd maxed out my credit card on the Florida trip. I had five dollars left in my pocket. And Big Blue guzzles gas faster than I can pump it in. I needed the capture money from Johnny.

"Good news and bad news," I said to Lula. "The good news is that they aren't dead. The bad news is that they're in Hawaii."

"That's what happens when you be a Good Samaritan," Lula said. "It's like ordering food at the drive-thru. You never know when they're going to short you on the fries."

TWENTY-THREE

I DROPPED LULA and Bob at the office and drove to my parents' house. Grandma was waiting at the door. I waved to her and she was off the porch and down the sidewalk before I had a chance to shut the engine off.

"I know where I want to go," Grandma said. "I went to one of them rescue websites, and I found a dog. The website said he was going to be up for adoption at the Petco store on Route 33. We gotta get there before someone else nabs him. I got my checkbook, my credit card, and $235 in mad money I've been hiding from your mother. I had more, but I spent it on the Florida trip."

"Is it a puppy?"

"Almost. He's four years old, but he looks like a puppy. He's white and brown spotted, and he has floppy ears. It said his name is Duffy, but I'm going to call him Henry. I always wanted a dog named Henry."

We walked into the store a couple minutes after it opened, and Grandma went straight to the adoption area in the front. There were several cats in cages and two small dogs. One of them was Duffy.

"What kind of dog is this?" I asked the attendant.

"He's a mix," she said. "He belonged to an elderly man who had to give him up when he went into a nursing home. If I had to make a guess I'd say he was part Maltese or Havanese."

"He's the one I want," Grandma said. "I saw him on your website, and I knew right away that he was the one."

"He's had all his shots and he's neutered," the woman said.

"How much does he weigh?" I asked her.

"Nine pounds."

"My pocketbook weighs more than that," Grandma said.

An hour later we were out of the store and back in Big Blue. Henry had a new red collar and leash, a dog bed, dog bowls, dog food, a bunch of dog toys, a dog toothbrush and toothpaste, a brush and comb, and a tag shaped like a dog bone with his name and Grandma's cellphone number on it.

"Does Mom know about this?" I asked Grandma.

"I might have forgot to tell her," Grandma said.

Henry was happy, sitting on Grandma's lap, and Grandma was looking out the window.

"There's another one of those protests up ahead," Grandma said. "I can't make out what they're protesting, but one of them looks like a zombie."

The protesters were in front of a new bakery, and one of the sign carriers looked like it might be the zombie version of Zero Slick. Under any other circumstances, I would have stopped, but I had Grandma and her new dog with me. And to further complicate things, Grandma was probably carrying and would like the chance to shoot a zombie.

I cruised past the protesters, and Grandma swiveled in her seat. "Do you think that was a real zombie?" she asked.

"No," I said. "I think it was someone made up to look like a zombie to get attention."

I parked in my parents' driveway, and I carried the bags of dog paraphernalia into the kitchen while Grandma walked Henry around the front yard, trying to get him to tinkle.

"What's all this?" my mom asked.

"Grandma has a surprise to show you," I said. "This is part of it."

Grandma brought Henry into the house. "Here he is," she said to my mom. "Isn't he a pip? His name is Henry, and he's not going to be any trouble. I'm going to walk him and feed him and he's going to sleep with me."

My mom's eyes glazed over for a beat, and I knew she was thinking Why me? "What on earth?" she finally said. "How. Why?"

I took the dog bed out of a bag and put it on the floor. "Because she was going to sleep with either Roger Murf and his wife, or else she was going to sleep with Henry."

My mom knelt down to get a better look at Henry. "He *is* cute," she said.

"I have to run," I said. "Things to do."

I wanted to get back to the protesters. I wanted to see the zombie up close. Hard to believe it could be Slick, but no stone unturned.

I hustled out of the Burg to the new bakery in Hamilton, and arrived just as the protesters were filing onto a bus. I parked and rushed over to a guy who looked like he was the handler.

"Is the zombie on the bus?" I asked him.

"Zombie?"

"Short guy with messy brown hair, wrinkled dirt-smudged clothes, red eyes. Smells like carnations."

"Ah, *that* guy. No, he took off on foot as soon as he got paid. We have another gig, but he wasn't interested."

"How much did he get paid?"

"Standard protester wage. Twenty dollars an hour for carrying a sign, and a twenty-dollar bonus if you heckle enough to start a riot. Why? Are you interested? I could use another body at the next stop."

"I could use the money. What will you be protesting?"

"I don't know exactly. I don't have the details on my work order. All I know is, it's a political fundraiser at a private residence."

"What were you protesting at this bakery?"

"They refuse to do gluten-free wedding cakes. It's blatantly discriminatory."

"I never thought of gluten in those terms."

"So, what's the word?" he asked. "Are you getting on the bus?"

"No, but thanks for the offer."

I returned to the Buick and drove a grid, looking for Slick. He was on foot. I thought he couldn't have gone far. After twenty minutes of searching I decided I needed another pair of eyes, so I went back to the office and got Lula.

"These zombies are sneaky," Lula said. She had her window down, hoping to catch a whiff of carnation. "One minute they're here and the next thing . . . poof."

I looked at my gas gauge. It was a smidgen from empty. By the time I dropped Lula at the bonds office, I'd be running on fumes. I drifted into a gas station and called Morelli while I pumped in my last twenty dollars.

"Have you gotten any forensics back?" I asked him.

"Yes. It's pretty interesting. I can't tell you everything over the phone, but we've been able to identify some of the DNA. The sample we got from the double-wide broken window was especially helpful. And the hot sauce on the take-out calf brains on my sidewalk was instantly identified as Tabasco. The red smear on your door also appears to be Tabasco."

Slick, I thought.

"Where are you now?" I asked.

"We're finishing up at Diggery's. We didn't find any zombies, but we found a second underground cave. And we made a good drug haul. That's all I can say."

"Bob is at the bonds office. I didn't want to leave him alone in your house."

"Thanks. I'm getting ready to head out. I'll pick him up on my way home."

"I think Slick is the Tabasco zombie. And for whatever reason he seems to be targeting me. I drove past a bakery in Hamilton Township this afternoon, and I thought I saw him with a bunch of protesters. By the time I got back to the bakery he was gone."

"We have a list of persons of interest, and he's on it. Tomorrow or Wednesday we'll have the lab report back on items we found today, and it should complete the picture. In the meantime, I'm thinking Mexican tonight. What's your pleasure? Burrito grande? Chicken fajita?"

"None of the above. I'm a zombie magnet. I don't want Slick coming back to your house. I'm going to stay at Rangeman. Ranger is out of town until midweek, and I can use his apartment. I've stayed there before and it's safe."

"I can handle Slick."

"Yes, but what happens when you aren't home? What happens when you get called out in the middle of the night because a headless corpse has been found at the multiplex?"

"Slick isn't a zombie."

"He's worse. He's a human who's acting and looking like a zombie. He's unpredictable."

"You're right," Morelli said. "I can't predict what he might do. I can't predict what any of these crazies might do. And you probably are safer at Rangeman for the next couple days. I can't guarantee that I'll always be here for you."

I was done pumping gas. It didn't take long to pump twenty dollars' worth. And Lula was gesturing to me from inside the car.

"I have to go," I said to Morelli. "Why don't I meet you for dinner?"

"There's a new place by the hospital. El Cheapo Pollo. Bad name but decent food. I ate there last week."

"Sounds good. I'll see you at six o'clock."

"I got the answer to our surveillance search problem," Lula said while I buckled myself in behind the wheel. "It's drones. What we need are drones, and I got a source. My friend Stump got a bunch of them that have cameras built in, and he's got one that's a heat seeker. He's on his way to meet us on the street behind the bakery."

Drones sounded like an okay idea. Sourcing them from a guy named Stump felt sketchy.

"Is this going to cost money?" I asked.

"No, but Stump says if we find a zombie he wants a selfie."

I drove to the bakery, circled the block, and parked. The bakery was on a busy street, lined with small businesses. The neighborhood behind the bakery was one of modest, neatly maintained single-family houses. The houses had small backyards and single-car garages. The buildings were bordered by mature shrubs and hedges. Lots of places for a short zombie to hide.

A jacked-up crew cab pickup truck pulled in behind me, and a middle-age balding guy swung out. His remaining hair was black and kinky curly. His skin was swarthy. He had a lot of tattoos, a thick Hispanic accent, and a body like a beer keg with legs.

"So, we hunting zombies today," he said to Lula.

"We know there's one sneaking around the neighborhood," Lula said. "We just can't find him, what with all the bushes and stuff."

"He gonna have no place to hide when I get my birds in the air. I'm putting my quadcopter up for you first. It'll stay up for almost a half hour and can cover four miles. I got a touch-control screen here so you can see what the bird sees and you can send it where you want it to go."

"I'd like it to search a grid, two blocks at a time," I said.

"No problem," Stump said. "She'll be up in a minute."

The picture came up on the screen, the four propellers started to whirl, and the drone lifted off the ground and rose to just above rooftop level.

"This is amazing," Lula said. "I need to get one of these. You could see everything. It's like I can fly."

"I'm cruising at a slow speed right now," Stump said, "but she can do forty miles an hour if I need to make a fast delivery."

"What do you deliver?" I asked him.

He looked at me like I had corn growing out of my ears. "Money. Drugs," he finally said. "And we use this in various locations to assess the movement of people."

"Stump's in the illegal immigration business," Lula said. "He's real good at it too. Nobody's ever died in any of his trucks."

"Everybody gets water, a blanket, and a granola bar," Stump said. "I run a first-class operation."

"I'm not seeing no zombie so far," Lula said. "Maybe Slick's already moved out of the area."

"I'll jump two blocks and make another sweep," Stump said. "Do you know what direction he's moving in?"

I shook my head. I didn't know.

"He's a zombie," Lula said. "He might want to get underground. He might be heading for a cemetery or a storm sewer."

"If he's one of them drug zombies he could be going to Morley Street," Stump said. "There's a guy distributes on Morley."

Whoa! "'Drug zombie'?"

"Yeah, there's some new street drug that turns people into zombies. Just popped up last week. At least that's when I heard about it. Goes by the name Zombuzz. Nasty stuff. I tried to get a piece of it, but it's a closed franchise."

"Do you know the distributor?" I asked.

"No. He's from out of town. I hear he's weird. They say he comes and goes like smoke. I don't even know what that means. Nobody knows much. Word is, he gives the stuff away. How do you compete with that?"

Stump's cellphone buzzed, and he read the text message.

"Sorry, ladies, gotta go," Stump said. "Business."

He tapped instructions to the drone and, in less than a minute, we could hear the high-pitched whine and see the quadcopter coming at us like a giant mosquito.

"I got it. I got it," Lula said, rushing toward the drone, arms outstretched.

The drone ticked off her fingertips and hit her on the forehead. *BONK!* Lula went still for a beat and then sat down hard on the ground.

"*Ow,*" she said.

I went to one knee beside her. "Are you okay?"

"Butterfly. Don't let them eat all the Fudgsicles."

Stump was packing his equipment. "You want me to put her in the back of the truck and drive her to the ER?"

Lula blinked at me and put her hand to her forehead. "What happened?"

"You tried to catch the drone, and it hit you in the head."

"Fucking drone."

"She's okay," I said to Stump. "I'll get her a bucket of chicken, and she'll be fine."

Stump drove away, and I helped Lula get into Big Blue.

"Did you know about the zombie drug?" I asked her.

"No. That's the first I heard. And usually I hear everything. What do you suppose happens to a zombie if he takes the zombie drug? Do you think he turns into a Fudgsicle?"

"Hang in there," I said to Lula. "I'm going to get you some chicken."

"Yeah, chicken would be good. And biscuits with gravy. And a Fudgsicle." Lula looked over at me. "Why do I keep saying 'Fudgsicle'?"

"Maybe you have a concussion. Do you want to go to the ER and get checked out?"

"No. I want to go to Cluck-in-a-Bucket and get some Fudgsicles."

"They don't have Fudgsicles at Cluck-in-a-Bucket," I said, "but I'm pretty sure they have them at the hospital."

"Then that's where I want to go."

TWENTY-FOUR

I DOUBLE-PARKED AND checked Lula in at the ER. Louise Burger was the admitting RN. I went to grade school with Louise, and one of my cousins was married to one of her cousins. I asked her to keep an eye on Lula while I ran an errand.

The office was several blocks from the hospital. I got there a little after four, just as Connie was shutting down for the day.

"I need an advance," I said to Connie. "I'm dead broke, and my credit card got maxed out when I had to bring Grandma back from Florida."

"What happened to Johnny Chucci?"

"Hawaii. I'm pretty sure he'll be back."

Connie unlocked the cash drawer. "How much do you need?"

"A hundred would be great."

She counted out a hundred and handed it over to me. "I got a new FTA an hour ago. The guy shouldn't be hard to find. First arrest. Not a lot of money involved, but it'll help until Chucci returns."

I took the file from her and paged through it. LeRoy Barker. Fifty years old. Looked all puffed up in his picture. Apple cheeks. Apple body. Wearing a three-button collared knit shirt that was two sizes too small. Self-employed electrician.

"Wow," I said to Connie. "This guy was arrested at his own birthday party?"

"Charged with drunk and disorderly. He's lucky he wasn't charged with assault. The party was at Chez Thomas on Route 33. LeRoy had a few too many cocktails, took all his clothes off, and fell asleep on the banquet table. When they tried to get him off the table he punched out the maître d'. Broke the guy's nose. It took six cops to wrangle LeRoy out of the restaurant and into a squad car."

"His address is listed as 25 Ferguson Avenue. That's right around the corner from Morelli."

"He's married and has two adult children," Connie said. "Both of the kids are out of the house, living on their own. The wife works at the button factory."

I tucked the file into my messenger bag. "I'm on it."

I chugged away in Big Blue, turned off Hamilton Avenue into Morelli's neighborhood, and parked behind LeRoy's truck on Cherry Street. His house was a small Cape Cod with two dormers in the front. No lights on in the house, but I could see the blue flicker of a television. I rang the bell, and LeRoy answered.

I introduced myself and explained to LeRoy that he'd missed his court date and needed to reschedule. I omitted the part that court was no longer in session so if I brought him in to reschedule he'd most likely be spending the night in jail.

"I'm depressed," LeRoy said. "I don't want to go to jail right now. I don't want to go out of the house. I don't *ever* want to go out of the house. I don't know what came over me. I was having a real good time, and then next thing I was naked and in jail. And now there's all these pictures of me online. I look like a beached whale. And if that wasn't bad enough, I passed out on the cake. My kids aren't talking to me, and my wife moved out."

"Jeez, that's horrible. I'm sure it's only temporary with your kids and wife."

"I could use a drink," LeRoy said.

"That might not be a good idea. How about a bucket of chicken? I have a friend in the ER. I have to go pick her up and buy her some chicken and biscuits. You could come along."

"Chicken might be good."

I looked at my watch. "I need to get back to her. Shut the television off and lock up your house."

"Am I going to jail?"

"Yes, but we're going to get chicken first."

Five minutes later I was once again double-parked in front of the ER entrance. I left LeRoy cuffed in the back seat, and I ran in to check on Lula.

"How's she doing?" I asked Louise.

"She's okay," Louise said. "She's finally stopped asking for a Fudgsicle. She has a minor concussion. Nothing serious. She's ready to be discharged."

I got Lula out of the building and buckled into the front seat.

"Hello, handsome," she said to LeRoy. "What's your problem?"

"He's FTA," I said. "I picked him up while you were in the ER. He's going for chicken with us."

"What did he do?"

"Drunk and disorderly," I said.

A loud sigh came out of the back seat.

Lula swiveled around and looked at him.

"I was stupid," LeRoy said.

"I bet I got you beat," Lula said. "I just got hit in the head by a drone."

"I drank too much and passed out naked on my birthday cake," LeRoy said.

"Did you face-plant?"

"I *everything* planted. It was a big sheet cake."

"You win. Did you at least get to eat some of it?"

"I don't think so. I can't remember. They hosed me off before they locked me up."

I swung into the drive-thru and ordered two buckets of chicken, two orders of biscuits with gravy, two extra-large sodas, and two apple pies.

"How come you're not eating?" LeRoy asked me.

"I have a date later," I said. "We're going to the Mexican place by the hospital."

Another sigh. "I ate there with my wife before she left me."

"Why did your wife leave you?" Lula asked.

"I embarrassed her when I passed out on my cake."

"That's it?"

"It was at Chez Thomas. And I was naked. And then I punched the maître d' in the face."

"Sounds like a good time to me," Lula said. "Any time you want to get naked and cover yourself with cake you just give me a call."

"Really?"

"Hell, yeah."

I parked in the Cluck-in-a-Bucket lot, unlocked LeRoy's cuffs, and distributed the food. By the time I reached the police station on the other side of town, Lula and LeRoy were working on their pie.

"I'll call you when I get out of jail," LeRoy said to Lula. "I don't think I want to pass out on my cake anymore, but we could go bowling or something."

"I'm up for that," Lula said. "I'm all about throwing big balls around."

I walked LeRoy into the station and turned him over to the cop at the desk.

"Sorry it's too late to bond you out today," I said to LeRoy, "but Connie will do it as soon as you see the judge tomorrow."

"Thanks for the chicken," he said. "I'm not so depressed anymore. And I like your friend Lula."

I got my body receipt and hustled across the street to Big Blue. I crawled along in rush-hour traffic, finally reached the office, and dropped Lula off at her car. I looked at my watch for the tenth time in fifteen minutes. I was late for Morelli. I circled a couple blocks, found a space, and attempted to parallel park the Buick. Impossible. I finally parked in the hospital garage and power-walked to the restaurant. Morelli was already seated.

"Sorry I'm late," I said to Morelli. "One of those days."

"Cupcake, all your days are 'one of those days.'" He stood and gave me a hello sort of kiss. "That's why I love you."

"You love me?"

"Yeah. You didn't know that?"

"It's nice to hear. I love you too."

Morelli grinned. "How *much* do you love me?"

"A medium amount."

"Really? Medium? Not a lot?"

"'A lot' might indicate impending marriage plans."

"We haven't got any of those."

"No."

He looked me over. "Weren't you wearing those clothes yesterday?"

I glanced down at myself. "I didn't get a chance to change. I was worried about zombies in the morning, and then things got congested in the afternoon."

"We could skip dinner and go straight to a shower and clean clothes. Or even better . . . no clothes."

"Tempting, but no. I'm starving."

"I ordered a pitcher of beer," Morelli said. "Hope that's okay."

"It's perfect. I need it *now*."

Morelli whistled through his teeth, and everyone jumped in the restaurant. He raised his hand and mouthed "Beer" to the waitress.

"Gee, that's smooth," I said to Morelli.

"I'm a Jersey Italian, and my girl needs a drink."

Both of these things were true.

The waitress brought our pitcher, we ordered off the menu, and I chugged my first glass.

"Okay, I feel better," I said. "I'm starting to relax."

"Your day was that bad?"

"Not bad. Hectic. Especially at the end. Lula got hit in the head by a drone, and I had to take her to the ER because she kept saying 'Fudgsicle.' While she was there I picked up a new FTA. Then I went back and got Lula."

"Is Lula okay?"

"Yes. Mostly she just needed a bucket of chicken."

"Where did the drone come from?"

"Lula had an idea to use a drone to look for Slick. It was actually a pretty good idea. The drone was amazing . . . until Lula tried to catch it, and it hit her in the head. It belonged to a friend of hers. Stump."

Morelli relaxed back in his chair. "Eugene Stump. The scourge of Trenton."

"I thought you were the scourge of Trenton."

"That was back in the day. Stump has a drone army. He uses the drones to move drugs and to help him move people."

"He said there's a new street drug called Zombuzz, and it turns users into zombies."

Morelli nodded. "The labs are still working, breaking it down, but we know the basics. It's a complicated synthetic mix that produces physical and psychological symptoms. Joints become stiff, making walking awkward. Chemical changes take place behind the eyes, and there's some bleeding involved. Users have no fear, feel no pain, have increased strength."

"What about the brain-eating thing?"

"We haven't apprehended a user yet, but from the physical evidence we've been able to retrieve, we think they aren't eating the brains. We think they're using them to manufacture the drug. We've found three underground caves that contain crude labs."

"So the dirty clothes and dirt-clogged hair, the red eyes, the classic zombie shuffle, all get explained by this drug and the way it's being manufactured?"

"In theory. We're still learning."

"Stump said it's being distributed by one man. He said the guy was from out of town and weird."

"It might have been the way it started, but I think it's moved beyond that now. Everything we've found points to multiple players producing product with widely varying degrees of purity."

"I'm surprised you haven't been able to round up some of these users."

"I can't arrest someone because his eyes are red and he shuffles. We have to wait for one of them to be caught committing a crime, or for one of them to overdose and end up dead or in the ER."

"What about DNA found on some of the victims? Were you able to identify any persons of interest?"

"Yes. We've interviewed two, and they made no sense. We have them under surveillance, and we're looking for a third."

I hated to ask the next question, but I couldn't help myself. "Were you able to identify anyone on the cemetery video?"

"It's disappeared. I had a tech working on it Friday. When

he came in today the camera was gone and his computer had been wiped clean."

I went numb for a couple beats. Diesel.

"How could that happen?" I asked. "It's a police station."

"That doesn't mean it's secure," Morelli said. "A lot of people have access."

The waitress brought corn chips and *queso*, and I dug into the chips, hoping to hide the fact that my heart was skipping around in my chest. Who the heck was I harboring in my apartment? Some guy who was able to break into a police station and wipe out a computer. Okay, calm down, I told myself. Maybe it wasn't Diesel. Like Morelli said, lots of people had access.

"On another note," Morelli said. "I saw the court docket for tomorrow, and Diggery was on it."

"I'd love to see him skate and get sent home. I don't want to be the long-term godmother to a fifty-pound snake."

"Evidence against him has been flimsy in the past. I'm not sure what they've got on him this time. And if he went to a jury trial I doubt there's anyone in Trenton who would convict him. He's like a folk legend."

. . .

It was a little after nine when I parked in Rangeman's underground garage and took the elevator to Ranger's apartment. I stood in the dimly lit hallway for a moment and let the cool air wash over me. I took a few calming breaths, listened to the silence, and felt my heart rate drop to a Zen level. His apartment had a sense of order that mine lacked. It was a good match with the man. They were both locked down in a way that gave the appearance of inner peace. I knew inner peace was an illusion for Ranger, but I also knew he believed if you practiced something long enough it became yours.

I went to the kitchen and said hello to Rex. He was on his wheel. Running, running, running. He paused, twitched his nose at me, and continued to run. I took my duffel bag into the bedroom and set it on a leather bench in Ranger's large walk-in closet. I had enough clothes for a couple days. Just the essentials. I knew from previous visits that Ranger was generous with his possessions. I could use his toiletries, raid his closet, eat his food, and drink his wine. And his housekeeper, Ella, was genius at providing forgotten essentials.

His bathroom was very masculine and spa-like. Carrara marble countertops. Pristine white tile on the floor and in the shower. Smoky gray paint on the walls. Endless steaming hot water. Bulgari Green shower gel that gave me a rush strong enough to buckle my knees when I soaped up because it smelled like Ranger.

I toweled dry and borrowed a black Rangeman T-shirt to use as a sleep shirt. I climbed into Ranger's bed and took a moment to enjoy the luxury. His sheets were soft and smooth, ironed by Ella. His pillow was perfect and lump free. His comforter was just right. If Ranger had been in the bed next to me I wouldn't have noticed any of these things. When you're in bed with Ranger, there's only Ranger.

TWENTY-FIVE

I WOKE UP at seven. It was dark in Ranger's bedroom, but light was streaming into the rest of his apartment. I padded barefoot into the kitchen and pressed the button on the coffee maker. Rex was burrowed deep in his soup can, sleeping off a hard night on the wheel. When Ranger is in residence Ella brings his breakfast at six A.M. House-smoked salmon from Tasmania, whole-grain toast, fresh fruit, yogurt. Sometimes he'll go nutty and put strawberry jam on his toast.

Ella knows that I sleep later and usually prefer to forage for my own breakfast. This morning I chose granola with fresh blueberries and strawberries.

I was at the kitchen counter, brewing a second cup of coffee, when I heard the apartment door open. A beat later, I heard keys get placed in the silver tray Ella kept on the hall table. Ranger was home.

He walked into the kitchen and kissed me. "Babe."

"I thought you weren't supposed to come home until later in the week."

"The job wrapped up early, and I was able to get a plane out this morning."

Ranger was dressed in black Rangeman fatigues. He was wearing a sidearm and a sheathed knife. All standard for men on duty. He almost always flew private, eliminating the hassle of airport security.

"Would you like me to call Ella for breakfast?" I asked him.

"I ate on the plane." The corners of his mouth tipped into a smile. "I like the way you look in my shirt."

I tugged at the hem. "It's a little short."

"I'd like it shorter."

My turn to smile. "It's nice of you to let me stay here. Rex and I appreciate it."

"Fill me in on the situation."

"You know about the zombies?"

"Yes."

"One or more seems to be stalking me," I said. "I thought it was a good idea to put myself in a safe place. And I didn't want to endanger anyone else . . . like the people in my building or my family."

"Tell me about the stalking."

I showed him the photos I'd taken of my door and Morelli's door.

"I think it might be Slick," I said. "There was discarded supermarket packaging left on Morelli's sidewalk along with a plastic fork. The label said 'calf brains,' and it had been doused with Tabasco. I know Slick is a Tabasco fan."

"I've been briefed on the drug the police believe is producing the zombie-like creatures. The chemistry of the drug alters brain function. Probably permanently. And it's highly addictive. A component of human brain is needed to produce the drug, so addicted users might be sent out to harvest brain. But from what I've read, there's no indication that a user would want to actually eat brain."

"So?"

"So, it's unlikely that your stalker would be a brain eater. I think it feels staged."

"No zombie?"

"Doubtful," Ranger said.

"Then who?"

Ranger's attention went back to the T-shirt. "I've missed you," he said. "You owe me some time."

Oh boy.

The smile returned. "Don't panic. It's just a game. You're the one who decides when we play."

That did me no good at all. Ranger was totally desirable. Being in a semi-committed relationship wasn't enough for me not to want Ranger. I would have to be dead. And even dead might not do it.

"Why isn't Diesel protecting you?" Ranger asked. "He's still in town."

"I never see him. He's looking for someone."

And that was the way I liked it. My biggest fear was that

Diesel would drag Slick into my apartment by the scruff of his neck, and I'd have to pay up on our deal and strip down.

"Diesel works for a little-known international organization that attempts to control exceptional people who go rogue," Ranger said. "Chances are good that he's looking for someone associated with the zombie drug. Maybe the chemist or biologist who developed it."

"What happens if *Diesel* goes rogue?"

"That would be a problem." Ranger took a bottle of water from the fridge. "I have to go downstairs. What are your plans for the day?"

"Simon Diggery is going before the judge today. I want to be there."

"Take a fleet car. I'll have Tank park it next to mine. He'll leave the key on the dash."

"Is this double or nothing again?"

"This one's on the house."

"Thanks. I'll try not to destroy it."

I took a shower, got dressed, and headed out. Tank had positioned a shiny black Honda CR-V next to Ranger's Porsche 911 Turbo. It was pretty and new, and just looking at it had my stomach in a knot. With me at the wheel, the poor thing was doomed to have an ugly end. It was only a matter of days. Maybe a matter of minutes!

I carefully eased the car out of the garage and drove to the office. Lula was at Connie's desk, shopping QVC on Connie's computer.

"Connie went to the courthouse to bond out LeRoy," Lula

said. "After he gets sprung, me and LeRoy are gonna meet for lunch."

"Diggery is in court today too. I called on my way here, and they said he's up for eleven o'clock. I thought I'd go over and see if he needs a ride home."

"You think he's gonna get off?"

"I'm hoping. I don't know why they keep arresting him. They can never make any of the charges stick."

"Yeah, but it slows him down," Lula said. "He stays clear of the cemetery for a while after he's been harassed."

• • •

Diggery saw me when he was led into the courtroom. It wasn't hard for him to spot me. There were only a few people scattered around. Judge Judy wasn't presiding, Bernie Madoff wasn't on trial, and no zombies were in attendance.

The sad sack before Diggery got thirty days for destruction of personal property while under the influence. He looked like he was under the influence a lot. The sad sack left, head down, and Diggery was called.

Diggery approached the bench, pleaded not guilty to the charges, and the judge looked like he wanted to hit himself in the head with his gavel. Probably this wasn't his first rodeo with Diggery.

Diggery went on to explain how he was doing volunteer gardening at the cemetery as part of a civic beautification campaign. And while he was digging so he could plant some geraniums he came upon a ring.

The judge gave up a sigh and told Diggery to speed things up.

"So anyways," Diggery said, "I put the ring in my pocket and forgot about it, what with the geranium planting and all. It didn't occur to me that it belonged to the lady resting in the grave. If it had been buried with her, how in holy heck did it get out of her slumber chamber?" Diggery leaned forward a little. "That's what they call the casket now," he told the judge. "Slumber chamber."

The judge did a small grimace. "Go on."

"I was leaving after my planting and one of our fine men in uniform, one of our wonderful first responders, mistook me for a miscreant. And that's how I came to be arrested."

"According to the arrest report, you were doing your gardening at two in the morning."

"That's right, your honor. That's when I do all my gardening. I got a touch of the skin cancer, so I garden at night."

The judge gave his head a small shake and looked at his watch. It was lunchtime. He looked at the prosecutor and the court-appointed public defender.

"Anybody? Anything?" the judge asked.

Nobody had anything.

"I'm fining you fifty dollars for trespass after cemetery hours," the judge said. "Do your gardening during the day and use sunscreen."

Diggery paid his fine, collected his belongings, and followed me across the street to the CR-V.

"Nice of you to give me a ride," he said. "Uber never wants to go down my street."

"There are some things you need to know," I said, pulling into traffic.

"I hope it's not bad news about Ethel."

"I haven't been to your double-wide today, but as far as I know, Ethel is fine."

"Then how bad can it be?"

"You know how we left the door open so Ethel could follow the hot-dog trail?"

"Yep."

"Well, a lot of raccoons got inside instead of Ethel."

"Again? Dang it. They keep doing that. Did they eat my peanut butter?"

"They ate everything. And then when they left, about a hundred cats went in."

Diggery nodded. "We got a mean pack of ferals in that neighborhood. Anything else?"

"One of the zombies smashed your window, but Ethel scared it off, and the police patched it up."

"Damn zombies."

"Turns out they aren't really zombies."

"I heard about it while I was in jail. You hear about everything in jail. They're drug zombies, and the only way they can get more of the drug is to pay for it with some human brain."

"That's sick."

"Doesn't seem to me like a good business plan. Why would you do it if you're not making any money on it?"

Diggery's street was blocked by a police cruiser, but we were waved through. There were more cruisers parked along the road, and Diggery's yard was being used as a staging area. Morelli's

SUV was there, as well as a police transport van. Diggery went straight to his double-wide to check on Ethel, and I went looking for Morelli. I found him behind the van, talking to a uniform.

"How's it going?" I asked him.

"So far we've rounded up three zombies."

"Are they in the van?"

"No. We've already transported them to the lockup at St. Francis for evaluation. When they're released from there, a bunch of three-letter agencies will take over."

"I brought Diggery home. He got fined for trespass, and he was told to do his gardening during the day from now on." I looked around. "Will you be here much longer?"

"The rest of the day. There's a lot of ground to cover. We have dogs in the woods and an eye in the sky."

I looked up at the helicopter hovering overhead.

"This is a big deal," I said.

"Yeah. Decapitation is unpopular. People don't like it. Using human brains to make mind-destroying drugs doesn't sit well either."

"Remember the deli container that was left on your sidewalk? Do you think that was a setup?"

"Yes. These druggies don't care about eating brains."

"Diggery says he heard in jail that the only way you can buy more of the drug is to pay with human brain."

"We've heard that, too. The first vial is free. After that you pay with brain."

"What's the point?"

"My guess is that someone thinks this is fun."

It was a chilling thought. It took insanity to a whole new level.

Diggery joined us.

"I want to thank you for taking such good care of Ethel," he said to me. "I know she can be a handful sometimes, but she's mostly a sweet old girl."

"I think your freezer supply of rats got eaten," I said.

"That's okay," Diggery said. "Plenty more where they came from."

I left Morelli and Diggery and drove to my parents' house to see how Grandma was doing with the new dog.

· · ·

Grandma and Henry greeted me at the door.

"I came to check on Henry," I said.

"He's a joy," Grandma said. "He's got perfect manners."

"He's got no manners," my mother yelled from the kitchen. "He barks at everything, and he pooped on the floor."

"He was nervous," Grandma said. "He only did that once."

Henry was wagging his tail and looking up at me with big brown eyes. I bent down to pet him, and he vibrated with happiness.

"He's a nice dog," I said to Grandma.

"We should take him for a walk," Grandma said. "I keep his leash right here on the sideboard, so it's always handy."

She hooked Henry up, and we walked him down the street.

"He's good on the leash," Grandma said. "He trots right along. And when he poops, it's little poops."

I love Bob, but Bob doesn't poop little poops.

We walked for several blocks and turned onto Judy Chucci's street. Judy was on her front steps, waving her arms and screaming. Johnny Chucci was in the front yard, smashing the gnomes with a hammer.

"You're killing them," Judy was screaming. "You're going to burn in hell."

"They're lumps of plaster," Johnny yelled back at her. "They aren't even interesting lumps. You suck at this. You need a new hobby. Try knitting. Try quilting. Try cleaning your house. It's a pigpen."

"I hate you. I hate you. I hate you," Judy shrieked.

"You're a fruitcake," Johnny said. "You're nuts. These stupid things aren't real." *SMASH.* Another gnome turned into plaster dust.

He went after the gnome with the blind eye, and even I had to cringe. It seemed excessive to attack Mr. Murphy.

SMASH. Mr. Murphy was sent to gnome heaven.

Judy disappeared into her house and returned with a chef's knife. "An eye for an eye," she said, charging after Johnny.

"He runs pretty good, considering that big bandage on his foot," Grandma said.

They ran past us, and I tackled Judy and took the knife away from her.

"Take Judy inside and make her a cup of tea or something," I said to Grandma. "I'm going to drive Johnny to the police station."

"I don't know if I want to go in that house with all them gnomes," Grandma said. "They kind of creep me out."

"They're house gnomes," Judy said. "They're very polite."

Grandma and Henry went inside with Judy, and I called Lula to pick me up. The bonds office was only minutes away.

"I thought you went to Hawaii on a pre-re-wedding honeymoon," I said to Johnny.

"I had plane tickets and hotel reservations, and we weren't on the plane more than fifteen minutes before it started about the gnomes. Mr. Murphy and little Susie and Grumpy. All the way to L.A. And then she wouldn't get on the connecting flight. She called her neighbor forty-five times. How were the gnomes? Was Mr. Murphy depressed? Who the hell is Mr. Murphy anyway?"

"You smashed him."

"Good. Now he's not depressed anymore."

Lula's Firebird pulled up to the curb.

"Jail is going to be a relief after this," Johnny said. "I can't wait to get locked up with some nice sane murderers and rapists."

"How's your foot?" Lula asked him.

"It's freaking killing me."

"I got some drugs in my purse," Lula said.

"Hand them over," Johnny said. "Mine are all on their way to Hawaii."

TWENTY-SIX

COURT WAS STILL in session when I turned Johnny over to the police, but he chose not to get bonded out again. He said he was exhausted, and he just wanted to sit in his cell and be happy he wasn't married. He said after he served his time and got released back into society, he was going to Hawaii and maybe he'd stay there.

"I totally get Johnny's point of view," Lula said, driving out of the municipal building lot. "Sometimes when you're whackadoodle you gotta find a place where you fit in with other whackadoodles. Not that I'm saying Hawaii is full of whackadoodles. I mean, I've never been there, but it seems like it's calling to Johnny Chucci."

The only thing *I* heard calling was lunch. I'd had a candy bar from the vending machine in the courthouse and nothing since.

"How did it work out with LeRoy?" I asked. "Did he make bond?"

"Yep. And we went to get something to eat after. We went to the deli on Line Street, and they have excellent coleslaw. You get a good dish of coleslaw, and it goes a long way at providing happiness for the rest of the day."

Words to live by.

"What about LeRoy?" I asked.

"He's confused," Lula said. "He doesn't know if his wife is coming back or not. I guess his kids got over him being naked on the cake, but the wife not so much. Sounds to me like they might have had problems before the cake incident. He's an okay guy, but I don't see a romantic future with him."

"Because of the wife confusion?"

"No. From what I can tell every married man has wife confusion. LeRoy is a tapper. Tap, tap, tap on everything. On the deli table. On the dashboard. On his chin. Only time he wasn't tapping was when you had him cuffed or when he got food in his hand. Only thing worse than a tapper is a jiggler or a hummer. You find a man does any of those things and you *run* don't *walk* away, because if you get locked in a room with him, eventually you're gonna have to kill him."

Lula stopped for a light, and I searched through my messenger bag, hoping to find a breakfast bar, finding only a cough drop.

I unwrapped the cough drop and popped it into my mouth. "Diggery got off with a fine this morning. Trespass at the wrong time of day."

"Connie told me. She said she heard from the court cop that

Diggery was on his game. Besides, everyone wanted to get out to the food truck. The Cuban sandwich guy was there today."

"I didn't know there was a food truck!"

"They let him park in the cop lot. Where were you parked?"

"Public parking across the street."

"You're such an amateur," Lula said. "You give the guy at the gate a BJ once in a while and he lets you park in the cop lot."

Not only did I not want to give the guy a BJ, but I had no confidence my BJ would be good enough for entrance into the lot.

"Anyway," I said, "I took Diggery home, and his neighborhood is filled with police rounding up zombies."

"I heard that too. Connie's sister-in-law works on the lockup floor at the hospital. She said the whole place stinks like carnations. Something about the chemistry of the drug that makes carnation stink ooze out of your skin. I have my own theory."

I was afraid to ask.

"I'm thinking that brains smell like carnations," Lula said. "Probably some people know that, like undertakers and doctors who do autopsies, but they don't tell nobody. That's why funeral homes always smell like carnations."

"They smell like carnations because people send flower arrangements with carnations in them."

"That's what they like you to believe," Lula said, "but downstairs they got dead people on slabs with their brains leaking out."

I turned the air-conditioning up and powered the window

down. I needed air. The cough drop wasn't sitting great in my stomach. Probably what I needed was bread. With meatloaf between it.

"I need to go to my parents' house," I said. "My car is there, and I want to make sure Grandma got home okay."

And there would be bread and meatloaf. And if no meatloaf, there'd at least be bologna.

Lula cut down a couple side streets and crossed the train tracks. Ten minutes later she turned into the Burg and pulled to the curb, behind my Honda SUV.

"Is this CR-V a new Ranger car?" she asked.

"Yes. It's a loaner."

"It's a shame it's gonna get destroyed by your bad car juju. It's freaky how the only car you can't kill is the Buick."

Freaky and depressing. The Buick drove like a refrigerator on wheels.

I waved goodbye to Lula and let myself into the house. I heard little dog feet running toward me, and Henry skittered around the corner and into the small foyer. He spun in circles and jumped against my legs. Grandma followed.

"We got a welcoming committee now," Grandma said. "Henry loves company."

"He tinkles on people," my mother shouted from the kitchen. "Don't let him near Stephanie."

"He gets excited," Grandma said. "It's only a little tinkle. He's mostly empty."

I picked Henry up and carried him into the kitchen.

"How did it go with Judy Chucci?" I asked Grandma.

"Pretty good, except her house is a mess. Gnomes everywhere. You can't hardly walk. Henry tinkled on a bunch of them, but she didn't notice, and I didn't say anything. I didn't think it mattered, what with the state of things."

"Is she going to be okay?"

"Well, she can fry up an egg and make coffee. Beyond that it's hard to tell. I told her she should take up bingo. It'll get her out of the house. She said Mr. Murphy would have loved bingo, even though he could see out of only one eye."

I put Henry down and went to the fridge. "Do we have any meatloaf?"

"Sit and I'll make you a sandwich," my mother said. "You look pale. Are you eating? You aren't living on candy bars, are you?"

"I try to get ones with nuts in them," I said, taking a place at the kitchen table. "Keeps my protein level up."

I couldn't see my mother's face, but I knew she was rolling her eyes and asking for help from whoever was working the help desk in heaven.

She gave me a meatloaf sandwich with chips and pickles. I broke off a small piece of meatloaf and fed it to Henry.

"We aren't feeding him at the table," my mother said.

"Of course, we are," Grandma said. "Look how little he is. Look how cute. And he was an orphan. Poor thing."

My mom pulled a chair out, sat down, and Henry jumped into her lap. Her shoulders slumped a little and she scratched him behind his ear. She was doomed. She was a sucker for kids and helpless little creatures.

I finished my food and called Morelli.

"I'm at my mom's," I said. "Do you need me to walk Bob?"

"No. I left Bob with my sister-in-law. I suspected I'd be late."

"How's it going with the zombie roundup?"

"We've gone through almost the entire area and cleaned out the underground dens. We'll stay here until dark and then pack it in. We haven't found any more zombies. Impossible to get a grip on the numbers. I'm sure the users are scattered."

"Why the underground dens? Why not abandoned buildings?"

"Don't know. Maybe we just haven't found the abandoned buildings. We have three users, but so far they're only talking gibberish."

"I don't suppose one of them was Slick?"

"Sorry. No."

"Do you have any more thoughts on the Tabasco zombie?"

"Yeah. I shouldn't be telling you this, but I think you need to know. They lifted Slick's fingerprints off the deli container."

It took a beat for me to catch my breath. "Do you still think it was a setup?"

"Yes. But I don't know why. It doesn't fit the user profile."

"Thanks for telling me."

"Be careful," he said.

I stood and stuffed my phone into my jeans pocket. I had an idea about the setup and Slick. He was making a video. It had started as a documentary, but now maybe he was fabricating. Maybe it had turned too ordinary when it became just another drug story. Maybe he had to sensationalize it. Problem was, I didn't know how far he would go to get good film. And I didn't know if he was using the drug. Bottom line was that I had to find Slick.

"Gotta go," I told my mom and Grandma. "I'm still looking for Zero Slick."

"If you find him, I wouldn't mind meeting him," Grandma said. "He's a real celebrity. He's the Zombie Blogger."

I felt my eyebrows lift halfway into my forehead. "How long has he been the Zombie Blogger?"

"Not too long. I started following him over the weekend. He's got some good videos on YouTube, too. He's making a real name for himself."

"I'd like to see some of his videos," I said.

"I got my computer on the dining room table," Grandma said. "All you have to do is look for Zero Slick."

I sat down, typed in his name, and there he was. The videos were all short. The cemetery during the day. Just scenery. The cemetery at night, badly lit, as if he was holding his cellphone camera with one hand, and a flashlight with the other. There were zombies in the night videos. Dirty, dull-faced creatures. Their gait was halting and stiff-legged. One of them fell into a pit that I assumed was an open grave. The camera cut away to another zombie sticking a needle into his arm.

More dark footage from inside one of the dirt caves. What appeared to be part of a head on a small table. Some surgical instruments also on the table. Sickening to look at given the atrocities of the past week. No sound with the video beyond some scraping and heavy breathing.

"He's good at making horror movies," Grandma said. "He has a real flair."

I didn't tell Grandma this was probably real. Better only one of us has nightmares.

The last two videos were my door with the words BRAINS and DIE scratched into it, and Morelli's vandalized door. Two blurred figures could be seen very briefly staring at Morelli's door. Morelli and me. I doubt anyone else would recognize us. The video had been shot from a distance, and the quality was poor.

"That's it for the movies," Grandma said. "According to his blog he'll be putting a new movie up tonight."

I took some time to read through his blog. It was a diary of his nighttime wanderings and adventures with the zombies. Hard to tell what was real and what was fiction. He wrote about working with the Supreme Ruler of the Zombies, and he promised that something shocking was about to be videoed.

I thought the videos I just watched were already *too* shocking. I wasn't a horror movie kind of person. I was more romantic comedy. Indiana Jones was as violent as I could go.

I called Morelli back.

"Have you seen Zero Slick's videos on YouTube?" I asked him.

"There are videos?"

"Yes. And he has a blog. You want to check it out. He mentions the Supreme Ruler of the Zombies. Apparently, they're hanging out together. And there's a fuzzy picture of us in front of your house, looking at your door."

"How did you discover this?"

"Grandma."

"I should have guessed," Morelli said.

I ended the call with Morelli, said goodbye to my mom, and walked to the door. Grandma went with me.

"Let me know if you need help with the zombies," Grandma said. "I'm good with dead people."

TWENTY-SEVEN

I DROVE OUT of the Burg and cruised past the bonds office. It was closed for the night. Traffic was heavy on Hamilton Avenue and going through the center of the city. Rush hour. Everyone going home. Except me. I was going to Rangeman. I drove into the garage, stepped into the elevator, and exited into Ranger's apartment. It was nice, but it wasn't home. I went to the kitchen and said hello to Rex and poured myself a glass of wine. Ranger kept wine in his apartment, but he almost never drank it. He didn't mix alcohol and guns. And he almost always carried a gun.

It was five o'clock. Ranger usually worked until six or six-thirty. Ella brought dinner at seven o'clock. I had time to kill. I took the wine into Ranger's office, settled into a leather club chair, and brought Slick's blog up on my computer. I read through it for the second time, and again the thing that stood out was his claim to be working with the Supreme Ruler of the Zombies. It smacked of a cheesy movie or a graphic novel. It was comic book stuff. Hard to take seriously. And yet, hard to ignore.

Someone had drifted into Trenton and set up shop to produce Zombuzz. That someone was an elusive entity. A freak who gave his drug away in exchange for human brains. And apparently he accepted brains that were mummified, embalmed, or fresh from the kill.

It was a little after six o'clock when I heard Ranger roll in. There was the *clink* of keys in the silver tray and soft footsteps in the hall. He smiled when he saw me in the chair with my computer.

"It's nice to find you here when I come home," he said. "I'd forgotten what it was like."

"Are you telling me you're lonely?"

"No. Just that I enjoy this once in a while."

I nodded. "Me too. I have something to show you. Zero Slick has a zombie blog, and he's uploaded some videos on YouTube."

"I've seen them. He needs better equipment."

"Do you think he's serious about working with the Supreme Ruler of the Zombies?"

"It's possible. He was in one of the caves. Someone took him there."

"Supreme Ruler?"

"It's a little Hollywood."

"Do you think there's a Supreme Ruler?"

"I think there's someone who brought the drug to Trenton, is controlling the distribution, and is enjoying the experience."

"Are you involved in this?"

"You're involved, so I'm involved."

"Do you think we should go proactive?"

"There are a lot of people working proactively. Morelli and his team are making good progress, considering the drug has only been here for two weeks, tops."

"Have you been in contact with Diesel?"

"Not directly. We see him moving around."

"Do you think he could be the Supreme Ruler?"

"No. He doesn't have that kind of ambition. He does his job because he's one of only a few people who have the skill. He didn't choose his job. His job chose him."

"Jeez. That's heavy."

Ranger shrugged. "He's a specialist. He has a decent amount of downtime, and he's well compensated."

"You know a lot about him."

"I was curious. I did some research."

A text message dinged on my phone. *It's showtime. You know where to find me. Midnight. Come alone or not at all. ZS.*

I showed the message to Ranger.

"Text him back and tell him midnight isn't going to work for you. Tell him you'll meet him at ten o'clock."

"Why ten o'clock?"

"I have an early meeting tomorrow. I don't want to be wandering around a cemetery until two in the morning."

"You think he's at the cemetery?"

"I assumed he was referring to the grave site where he was camped out. That was where you met him when his video career began."

"How do you know about that meeting?"

"I have a transmitter in your messenger bag, and another attached to whatever car you're driving. And we monitor the police band."

"Yep. That would do it."

I texted Ranger's message to Slick, and got a response back that ten o'clock would be okay.

· · ·

Ella delivered dinner at seven o'clock. Grilled snapper, asparagus, soft polenta. Fresh fruit for dessert. Delicious but not up to Cluck-in-a-Bucket standards. No rancid grease. No sugar-fortified apple pie. No bacon, full-fat cheese, or deep-fried onion rings.

I finished my fruit and stared down at my empty plate.

"Babe," Ranger said. "You look like you'd kill for a cookie."

That had me smiling. "A cookie would be good, but I wasn't thinking about a cookie. I was thinking about Zero Slick. I have a sick feeling that he wants me to play a role in the shocking new video he promised his viewers."

Ranger's phone buzzed, and I saw a picture come up on the screen. I thought Ranger's initial reaction was annoyance, but that fast changed to amusement. He didn't smile, but the corners of his mouth tipped up a little. I'd produced this same reaction from him on many occasions.

"Send him up," Ranger said.

He turned his phone so I could see the screen. It was Diesel. He was relaxed, thumbs hooked into his jeans pockets, smiling up at the elevator camera.

"We have company," Ranger said.

"Was he invited?"

"No. But he's not unexpected."

Ranger opened the door to Diesel, and we all went into Ranger's office.

"Long time, no see," I said to Diesel.

"Yeah, I haven't had much social time on this trip."

He slouched into a club chair, I sat in the second club chair, and Ranger sat at his desk. Ranger was chairman of the board. If it came to a power struggle between the two men, I couldn't predict a winner.

"I assume we're looking for the same man," Ranger said.

Diesel nodded. "I should have wrapped this up by now, but there are qualities to this person that make him hard to track. And now I have an additional problem. The police are shutting down his playground, and if he stops having fun, he'll pack up and move on. If that happens, I'll have to start over."

"Is this his first playground?" Ranger asked.

"No. He was in Berlin for a short time, and then he moved to Atlanta. This time I have a better shot at catching him because he's chosen to hang out with Zero Slick. And Zero Slick isn't smart."

"Who are we looking for?" Ranger asked.

"His name is Daryl Meadum. He's brilliant but childlike.

He's a savant. And he's a sociopath. He's Canadian born. He has an American passport. He speaks five languages."

"Do you have a photo?" I asked.

Diesel pulled a photo up on his phone.

Daryl Meadum had an impish grin, pale skin with freckles, and red to blond hair cut short. He was a nice-looking kid. Maybe fourteen. And I was pretty sure he was the boy I saw on Diggery's road.

"How old is he?" I asked.

"Thirty-two."

"He looks like he's fourteen."

"That's part of the problem. People tend not to notice kids. And Daryl looks like apple pie. He's soft-spoken. He appears shy. He exists in shadows. He's always pleasant. He also has heightened senses and instincts like a cat.

"He isn't capable of feeling remorse, unless it's for losing a video game. His emotional age would be somewhere between nine and twelve. His passion is neuroscience. He's held research positions at various universities since he was eighteen years old. For the last seven years he's been working for the government. I'm told his knowledge and insight make him irreplaceably valuable. He has handlers who make sure he doesn't starve or walk in front of a train or kill someone as a scientific experiment.

"Daryl slipped away from his guardian and disappeared from a conference in Munich four months ago. When a new street drug surfaced that was based on brain cells, I was called in to find Daryl."

"And you think Daryl is the Supreme Ruler of the Zombies," I said.

Diesel grinned. "Yeah. He loves zombies, vampires, superheroes, werewolves. His dossier says he wears Power Rangers underwear."

"Why does he need an underground cave to make his drug?" I asked.

"He doesn't," Diesel said. "He's playing. You need to think like a nine-year-old boy. His drug makes zombies. Burrowing underground and playing hide-and-seek in a cemetery is part of his zombie play."

"How does he survive?" I asked. "Where does he live? How does he get food? All that costs money. Where does he get money?"

"He steals. He cons. He hacks into systems. He improvises," Diesel said. "And right now, he has Zero Slick to help him."

"Two mental twelve-year-olds with delusions of fame," Ranger said. "Engaged in role-playing."

"Exactly," Diesel said. "Daryl's role is Supreme Ruler of the Zombies. It's not clear if he knows he's pretending or if he thinks he really *is* the Supreme Ruler. Slick is easier. He's convinced he's making an award-winning video."

"His blog promised a new shocking video tonight, and he just asked me to meet him at the cemetery at ten o'clock. I'm worried he has video plans for me."

"I've seen those videos," Diesel said. "They need help. Smart of him to realize he needs to spice things up with a pretty girl."

Being part of Slick's video was sort of a depressing turn of events. On the other hand, Diesel thought I was pretty.

"He wants me to come alone," I said. "How could he possibly believe I'd do that? He wants me to meet him at night in a cemetery that's rampant with zombies."

"He's a YouTube sensation," Diesel said. "In his mind, any woman would jump at the chance to be part of his video. And either he looks at you as a stupid, inferior female, or else you represent power and you would be stupidly fearless. Either way, you would think nothing of meeting him in a cemetery late at night."

Jeez Louise. Now I was really depressed.

"This is good," Diesel said. "We know where to find Slick. And if we find him, there's hope that we can find Daryl. There's even a decent possibility that Daryl might be on hand for the video."

I was trying not to think too much about the video. I suspected it involved my brain.

"I can put a few key men in the cemetery, and I can put a drone in the sky," Ranger said to Diesel. "I'm afraid if we involve the police there will be too much presence."

"What about Stephanie?" Diesel asked.

Ranger looked at me. "Stephanie speaks for herself."

Oh great. It was going to be my decision to risk my brain for the cause. The way I saw it I was going to look like an idiot if I was in, and I was going to look like a jerk if I wasn't.

"Babe?" Ranger said.

I blew out a sigh. "I'm in. What's my role?"

Diesel grinned. "You have a choice. You can be the stupid inferior female or the stupid powerful female."

"How about if I'm just myself?"

267

Diesel glanced at Ranger. "I'm not going to touch that one."

Ranger shook his head. "I'll pass."

"Funny," I said. "Very funny."

"I'll put a wire on her," Ranger said to Diesel. "Come down to the control room with me, and I'll get you equipped to communicate with the rest of the team."

From the little I knew about Diesel I thought he probably didn't need the equipment. Diesel wasn't normal. It wouldn't surprise me if he read minds and could stick a lightbulb in his mouth and light up a room.

TWENTY-EIGHT

RANGER RETURNED TO his apartment a little before nine. He was holding a wire and a roll of surgical tape.

"Time to get dressed," he said, setting the wire and the tape on a kitchen counter.

The device itself was small. About the size of a dime. State-of-the-art. I'd been wired before, so I knew what to expect. And because Ranger was placing the wire I knew what to expect there too.

I was wearing jeans and a stretchy V-neck T-shirt.

"I can do this," I said. "Just give me the wire. I know where it goes."

Ranger put his hands on my waist and drew me closer. "That wouldn't be as much fun."

I narrowed my eyes at him. "There will be no *fun*. I'm in a relationship."

"Don't worry. I'm a professional. I've done this before."

His hands were under my shirt, skimming over my rib cage, lifting my shirt.

"Wait," I said.

Too late, the shirt was over my head. A heartbeat later he'd unclasped my bra and his hands were on me. They were warm and familiar, at the small of my back. He brushed a light kiss across my lips, and I got a rush all the way to my toes.

I was doomed. "Oh crap," I said.

I could feel Ranger smile. "Babe," he said in a whisper.

. . .

My clothes were scattered around the kitchen, and Ranger was trying to tape the wire to me.

"It's not sticking," I said.

"It's because you're sweaty."

"It's *your* sweat," I said. "I don't sweat. Ladies don't sweat."

"Babe, you're no lady."

I knew that was a compliment and a comment on the last twenty minutes. Truth is, if Slick and the Supreme Ruler of the Zombies suck out my brain tonight at least I'll have had this one last cosmic orgasm.

I took a fast shower and got dressed in clean clothes. We got the wire on me in seconds, and we were out the door. I was driving my Rangeman CR-V and Ranger was beside me. Tank was following in another Rangeman SUV.

"My men are in place," Ranger said. "And Diesel is out

there . . . somewhere. If you get into trouble we can reach you in seconds. The goal is to capture Daryl. Hopefully he'll show up. If he doesn't show, you're going to be on your own to make it happen. Remember the code word for us to move in is 'red sky.'"

"Right. Got it. Red sky."

I stopped two blocks from the cemetery parking lot, and Ranger got out and moved to Tank's SUV. I continued on, trying to ignore the churning in my stomach. I was five minutes early when I parked. I had a stun gun in one sweatshirt pocket and a small canister of pepper spray in the other. My cellphone was in my jeans pocket. When I killed the lights, I was enveloped in darkness. I left my messenger bag on the back seat and got out of the car. I stuffed the keys into another pocket of my jeans. I stood for a moment, waiting for my eyes to adjust to the darkness. I saw lights turn into the driveway that led to the lot. Not an SUV. They were too low to the ground. The car swung into the lot and parked next to me. It was Lula.

"Hey, girlfriend," Lula said, getting out of the Firebird, locking up. "I see you got an invitation too. Good thing I just got my nails done, except I don't know if they're gonna show up in the dark. The text message was short. It didn't say if there was going to be lights set up. Most of Slick's videos only have atmospheric lighting, like from a flashlight."

Lula was wearing a short, skintight, low-cut dress that was entirely bedazzled. Even in the dark, the dress was blinding. Her five-inch stilettos matched the dress, and she had silver glitter on her eyelids.

"This could be my moment," Lula said, tugging her dress down over her ass.

"Do you really think he wants to make a video?"

"Well, yeah, what else would he want? He's got a questionable sexual identity, so I don't think this is going to be a romantic liaison. I got an idea for putting music to the video. Something sexy with a good strong beat. Like club music, you see what I'm saying?"

"I was a little worried that he might want my brain."

"He didn't say nothing about that in my text message. And that better not be the case because my brain's staying in my head, right where it belongs."

I knew Ranger and Tank were listening in on this conversation. It took a lot to make Ranger laugh out loud, but I figured this had him doubled over.

Lula hauled a Maglite out of her purse and flashed it on. So much for the stealth approach.

"Let's do this," Lula said, setting off for the gate that led to the footpath. "Showtime."

"I thought you didn't like cemeteries."

"Yeah, but I'm willing to make an exception for my chance to be a video star. It's not every day something like this comes along."

This was true.

We walked along the footpath and spotted Zero Slick sitting on a tombstone, exactly where I'd expected to find him. He seemed to be alone. He wasn't quite as scruffy and zombie-like as the last time I saw him. Probably because Morelli had shut down the dirt dens.

"Here we are," Lula said. "What's the plan? Do you have a script? Are there any other people coming? I thought by now you might have a crew."

"I like to do my own camerawork," Slick said. "That way I have total control."

"For a while there when you disappeared, we thought you might have turned into a zombie," Lula said.

"I was thinking about it, but then I decided that wasn't my destiny. I was meant to make videos and to blog."

"Good for you," Lula said. "And I suppose you remembered that I had some extensive experience in front of the camera."

"Sure," Slick said, "but mostly I need you for diversity. That's the key word these days. Diversity. If I want to get recognized as a great filmmaker I need to have some diversified zombies. Right now, I only have white zombies."

"Hunh," Lula said, hands on her hips. "Are you telling me I been invited because I'm gonna be your token diversification goddess?"

"Yes."

"Okay then, now that we got that straightened out. I'm still getting a producer credit, right?"

"Right."

"So, it sounds to me like you want us to be zombies," I said to Slick.

"Totally. And apologies because ordinarily we would have done this filming in one of our zombie transformation dens, but we're currently relocating."

"Who is 'we'?" I asked.

"I bet I know," Lula said. "I bet it's the Supreme Ruler of the

Zombies. I've been reading your blog, so I know you guys have been hanging together." Lula swept her flashlight beam around the grave site. "Where is he? Is he here?"

"He's in the area, but he never allows anyone to see him. Only zombies and, of course, me."

"Well, I want to see him," Lula said. "I got all dressed up for this gig."

"You can see him after you become a zombie," Slick said.

"I guess that's okay," Lula said. "I don't mind putting some makeup on, but I don't want to smudge up my dress. I'm not gonna be that kind of zombie. I'm Glam Zombie."

"Are we going to be filming here?" I asked Slick.

"Not exactly. There's a new grave site toward the back of the cemetery. Someone's getting interred tomorrow, and the fresh-dug grave will be awesome for the video."

"I heard they rounded up a bunch of zombies," Lula said. "Do you still got enough to film?"

"Trust me, there's no shortage of zombies. We're always recruiting new ones."

Slick led the way along the path, and I pulled Lula aside.

"You know there really aren't zombies, right? Slick and the Ruler are distributing a drug that gives people the characteristics of a zombie."

"Yeah, but they look like zombies. They just aren't totally dead yet. I mean, I've seen some of them, and they're real close to being dead. And they got a focus on getting brains . . . just like a zombie."

I couldn't argue with any of this.

We followed Slick to the far edge of the cemetery. Lula's

heels clicked on the paved footpath. Her Maglite flicked side to side.

"Tell you the truth," she said to me. "I'm getting a little freaked. I'm thinking there might be ghosts here besides zombies. I'm pretty sure I can feel them slithering against my skin. I got the creepy-crawlies."

I had the creepy-crawlies too, but mine were coming from Zero Slick.

Slick stopped at a spot that had a tarp stretched over a mound of earth and another over an open grave. He pulled the tarp away from the grave.

"Here's the scene," Slick said. "You jump in, and we film you down there looking like you're climbing out. You have to look like you're coming out of the zombie portal."

There was no way in hell I was going into the grave. And I know it was my civic duty to help catch Daryl the sociopathic drug lord, but I wasn't feeling it. I was thinking this was a bad idea, and I would rather be back in Ranger's apartment, or Morelli's house, or even my own apartment. I was thinking some moronic television show and a glass of wine would be good.

"I got on my special bedazzled Via Spigas," Lula said. "These aren't no grave-jumping shoes. How about if I just run around and wave my arms in the air and look batshit scared?"

"I guess that would be okay," Slick said. "I could get some footage of that."

"Hold on," I said. "We aren't doing anything until the Supreme Ruler shows up."

"Why not?" Slick asked.

"Because that's the way it is," I said. "It's not like we're a couple extras in some second-rate video. We expect to work with top people."

"And what about your fans?" Lula said. "They deserve to see the big guy, Mr. Supreme."

"Don't worry about my fans," Slick said. "I promised them a shocking video, and I'm going to deliver. I have it all planned out."

"I think you're full of baloney," I said to him. "I think you made it up about the Supreme Ruler. I think you're making a fake documentary."

"I'm making the documentary of the century," Slick said. "You should be begging me to let you jump in the hole."

"You got delusions," Lula said. "You're a deluded person."

"You said the Supreme Ruler is in the area. Exactly where is he?" I asked Slick. "Is he at Mickey's eating cheese fries? Is he wandering around, reading tombstones?"

"He's with the army," Slick said. "He'll come with the army when I give the signal."

"What army is that?" Lula asked.

"The zombie army," Slick said.

"I bet you got a zombie navy too," Lula said. "And a zombie air force."

"Not yet," Slick said. "Just the army. They've been gathering while we've been talking. They're going to help with the final scene."

I looked beyond him, and I saw two red eyes glowing in the dark night. A second later more red eyes blinked on.

"What the heck?" Lula said. "Are you kidding me?"

She panned with the Maglite and the zombies groaned and

swayed side to side when the light hit them. They were armed with shovels and hatchets.

"You're surrounded," Slick said. "Just like an apocalypse." He had a small video camera and he started filming the advancing zombies, and then he focused on Lula and me. "Jump into the grave," he said. "If you don't jump into the grave, they'll hack you to death. You'll be safe in the grave."

The zombies were shuffling forward. When they weren't caught in the light beam it was too dark to see anything other than the glowing eyes.

"Red sky," I said. "Red sky. Get me out of here. I'm done. I don't care that the crazy guy isn't here. Red sky. Red sky."

"What's with the red sky?" Lula asked.

"I'm wired. I'm calling Ranger in to get us out of here."

I pulled the neck of my T-shirt out and looked down at the wire. It wasn't there. I slipped my hand under my bra and came up with a single strip of loose tape. No wire.

"Stupid tape," I said.

"I don't like the sound of that," Lula said.

"The tape came loose and the wire fell off."

"Help!" Lula yelled.

TWENTY-NINE

SLICK RUSHED AT Lula, and shoved her backward. She lost her balance and fell into the grave. It was about seven feet deep, and she landed with a *thud*.

"Oh crap," Lula said. "Lordy, Lordy."

I pulled my stun gun out, but I was grabbed from behind before I could power up. I kicked back and tried to wrench free. A second set of hands was on me. I was yanked back and tossed into the grave. I scrambled to my feet and started to shout for help.

"That's good," Slick said. "Claw at the dirt like you're trying to climb out. And it would be great if you could cry."

The zombies were lined up around the grave.

"Commence shoveling," Slick said. "We need to bury them alive."

"Excuse me?" Lula said.

Slick looked down at us. "We're not going to totally bury you alive. We're going to leave your head sticking out because the Supreme Ruler wants your brains. It's another part of the diversity movement. Brain diversity."

I shouted for help, and I was hit in the face with a shovelful of dirt. All the zombies were shoveling. They were moving the dirt that had been piled alongside the grave back into the grave.

"I gotta get out of here," Lula said. "Give me a boost up. I'm gonna take out some zombies."

I leaned against the dirt wall, and Lula climbed up me as best she could. A zombie swung his shovel at her, she grabbed the shovel, and pulled the zombie into the grave with us. He was on his back, flapping his arms, grunting, unable to roll over. The other zombies shoveled dirt over him. They were shoveling like robots without direction or emotion.

I ducked my head to avoid the dirt flying at me, and I shouted for help. Floodlights flashed on, and there were men in uniform everywhere. Some were Rangeman guys, and some were police. Ranger dropped into the grave and brushed dirt off my head.

"Are you okay?" he asked.

"I lost the wire. It was the stupid tape."

"Sorry. It put us at a disadvantage. Fortunately, I had a drone up, and we were at least able to see what was happening on the ground. I would have moved in sooner, but I decided it was best to involve the police when I saw the number of zombies."

"Slick said Daryl was here, but he wouldn't show his face until Lula and I were zombies. Turns out, the plan was to bury us alive and take our brains."

"That wasn't going to happen. Diesel and I were ready to go in and snatch you out. We were just waiting for everyone to get into place."

Morelli was standing on the edge of the grave. Ranger lifted me up, and Morelli grabbed me and set me on my feet.

"What about me?" Lula said.

Lula was two inches shorter than I was and about seventy-five pounds heavier.

Ranger looked at her and grinned.

Morelli was also grinning. "I'm game if you are," he said to Ranger.

Ranger hoisted Lula up to Morelli, and Morelli took it from there. To their credit, neither of them broke a sweat or grunted with the exertion. Lula's skirt was up around her waist by the time she was set on the ground, and we were all treated to a view of her purple satin thong.

"I got dirt all over my bedazzled dress," Lula said. "And my shoes are ruined."

The police were cuffing all the zombies, and Diesel had Slick in tow.

"I found him," Diesel said to me. "Break out the deck of Old Maid cards."

I shoved my stun gun back into my pocket. "It doesn't count. I found him first."

"Yeah, but I *caught* him."

"What's this about?" Morelli asked.

"You don't want to know," I told him. "And anyway, it's about *nothing.*"

"We'll see," Diesel said.

Lula speared Slick in the foot with her stiletto heel.

"Oops, sorry," she said. "I'm so clumsy. I didn't see your foot sticking out there like that." She speared his other foot. "Or that one either," she said.

"Police brutality," Slick said.

"I'm not no cop," Lula said. "I'm a former 'ho and now I'm doing some clerking."

"I'd like to talk to the Supreme Ruler," Diesel said to Slick. "How about you take me to him."

"I can't do that," Slick said. "He comes to me. I never know where he is."

Diesel picked Slick up by his ankles and held him at arm's length over the grave.

"Does this help?"

"I don't know. I swear. He's spooky. All of a sudden he's standing behind me, and then he's gone."

Diesel brought Slick in and dumped him on the ground. "All yours," he said to Morelli.

Morelli and Ranger were busy doing cleanup, and Diesel disappeared, presumably looking for Daryl. Lula and I walked back to the parking lot.

"Here's another night of my life I won't get back," Lula said. "I'm going home. I'm going to put my jammies on and watch a movie. It's not gonna have zombies in it either. I'm done with zombies."

Going home sounded like a good idea. Slick was in custody and I'd get my recovery money. I had nothing to fear. Morelli would be busy for hours. And I had no justification for staying with Ranger. I was already feeling the adrenaline letdown. I wanted to crash into bed and sleep for days.

I drove back to my apartment on autopilot. I managed to get myself into the elevator and down the hall. I plugged my key into the lock, opened the door, and flipped the lights on. Home sweet home. I went straight to my bedroom and kicked my shoes off. I stripped my shirt off and heard someone giggle behind me.

Daryl Meadum, the kid I saw on Diggery's road, was standing in my doorway, holding a gun.

"I see you in your underwear," he said.

"What are you doing here? How did you get in?"

"I'm brilliant. Opening doors is a snap for me."

"Shouldn't you be relocating?"

"Yes, this is my last stop in Trenton."

He was speaking so softly I had to strain to listen.

"I need a healthy culture to take to my new location. Frequently brain cells that are made available to me are inferior and produce an inferior product. Cadaver brain cells, for instance, are never my first choice. It's difficult to build a good zombie army with inferior product."

"Why do you want to build a zombie army?"

"It's fun. It's much more fun than video game zombies."

"Don't you miss doing your research?"

"No. It was boring. And people were always watching me, ordering me around. *Eat your vegetables. Change your socks. Time for bed. Don't do a lobotomy on the cat.*"

I was feeling a little weirded out, standing in my bra, talking at gunpoint to the Supreme Ruler of the Zombies. Especially since he looked like he was fourteen years old. I was hoping I could distract him with conversation and create an opportunity to snatch the gun away. He didn't look comfortable holding it. I suspected he had little to no shooting experience.

"It isn't necessary to keep the gun pointed at me," I said. "We're friends, right?"

"Actually I have to kill you, so I can get your brain. I don't usually do the killing, but this is the most efficient way to go about it. I brought my tools with me in my backpack. I have a power drill and a small power saw, so I have options. Probably I'll go with the saw. It will allow me to remove the whole brain intact. I'm completely prepared. I have an insulated bag and an ice pack."

"Gross!"

"Not at all. It should be an interesting experience. I like that you've removed your shirt. It feels very naughty to be killing you when you're only wearing a bra. I don't suppose you'd want to take it off?"

"I'll trade you my bra for your gun."

He thought about it for a moment. "That wouldn't be a smart trade," he said. "I can remove your bra after I kill you. In fact, I might remove all your clothes after I kill you."

Eeek. Instant nausea. I swallowed back the revulsion and caught a glimpse of motion behind Daryl. It was so fleeting I thought I might have imagined it.

"So," I said to Daryl, "where are you going next?"

"Austin," he said. "I hear they have a good club scene. I think I can recruit some interesting zombies there."

Diesel moved in behind Daryl. "Austin isn't an option," Diesel said.

Daryl spun around and pointed the gun at Diesel. "It *is* an option. I do what I want now. You have no control over me. If you don't leave I'll shoot you."

"First off," Diesel said, "I have total control over you, and your days of doing what you want are over. Second, if you shoot me it's really going to piss me off, and you don't want to piss me off."

"I could kill you," Daryl said.

"I'm not that easy to kill," Diesel told him. "You should know that. Give me the gun."

Daryl squeezed off a shot that hit Diesel in the leg, about three inches above his knee.

Diesel looked down at the hole in his jeans and shook his head. "This is getting old," he said. "This is the second time I've been shot this week."

"I meant to shoot you in the heart," Daryl said, "but I'm not used to this gun. Hold still while I try again."

I grabbed the lamp off my bedside table and took two giant steps closer to Daryl. Daryl turned toward me, I whacked him in the face with the lamp, and he crumpled to the floor.

Diesel stood with his hands on his hips, looking down at Daryl. Blood was gushing from Daryl's nose onto his shirt and my bedroom carpet, and his eyes had rolled back into his head.

"Nice," Diesel said.

"Did I kill him?"

Diesel nudged Daryl with his foot, and Daryl moaned.

"Nope," Diesel said. "Not dead. Mostly you just rearranged his face."

Daryl blinked to focus his eyes.

"I had a good run," Daryl said.

Diesel nodded. "You had a good run."

"And I saw her in her underwear," Daryl said.

Diesel grinned. "Something to remember."

Diesel hoisted Daryl to his feet and held him steady. Blood was still dripping from Daryl's nose, but it had slowed to a trickle. Diesel's jeans were caked with blood where he'd been shot.

"Are you okay?" I asked Diesel. "You need to get to the ER. You have a bullet in you!"

"Yeah," Diesel said. "And digging it out is always a bitch."

"Always? How many times have you been shot?"

"Occupational hazard," Diesel said. "Not a big deal. I'm a fast healer."

"Me too," Daryl said. "Do I still have a nose?"

"I have to turn Daryl over to the appropriate agency," Diesel said. "I'll get looked at by a medic in transit. And I'll be back after I deliver Daryl. We have unfinished business."

"Me too," Daryl said. "I'll be back, too."

"Not on my watch," Diesel said.

"Your watch will end," Daryl said. "My life work will continue."

I stopped Diesel at my front door and pulled him aside. "Do I have to worry about Daryl coming back?" I asked him.

"No," Diesel said. "You have to worry about *me* coming back. I'm batshit lucky at Old Maid."

ABOUT THE AUTHOR

JANET EVANOVICH is the #1 *New York Times*-bestselling author of the Stephanie Plum series, the Fox and O'Hare series, the Lizzy and Diesel series, the Alexandra Barnaby novels (including the *Troublemaker* graphic novel), and *How I Write: Secrets of a Bestselling Author.*

Evanovich.com

Facebook.com/JanetEvanovich

@JanetEvanovich

ABOUT THE TYPE

This book was set in Minion, a 1990 Adobe Originals typeface by Robert Slimbach (b. 1956). Minion is inspired by classical, old-style typefaces of the late Renaissance, a period of elegant, beautiful, and highly readable type designs. Created primarily for text setting, Minion combines the aesthetic and functional qualities that make text type highly readable with the versatility of digital technology.